EYES OF THE
EMPEROR

ALSO AVAILABLE FROM
LAUREL-LEAF BOOKS

GRAHAM SALISBURY

EYES OF THE
EMPEROR

LAUREL-LEAF BOOKS

Published by Laurel-Leaf
an imprint of Random House Children's Books
a division of Random House, Inc.
New York

Originally published in hardcover in the United States by
Wendy Lamb Books, New York, in 2005. This edition published
by arrangement with Wendy Lamb Books.

Laurel-Leaf and colophon are registered trademarks
of Random House, Inc.

www.randomhouse.com/teens

Educators and librarians, for a variety of teaching tools,
visit us at www.randomhouse.com/teachers
RL: 5.0
ISBN: 978-0-440-22956-8
January 2007
Printed in the United States of America
10 9 8 7 6 5 4 3

THIS WORK IS DEDICATED
TO THE "BOYS OF COMPANY B"
WHO SERVED ON CAT ISLAND, MISSISSIPPI,
DURING WORLD WAR II:

Robert Goshima, Masao Hatanaka,
Noboro Hirasuna, Masao Koizumi, Herbert Ishii,
Fred Kanemura, James Komatsu, Masami Iwashita,
John Kihara, Katsumi Maeda, Koyei Matsumoto,
Toshio Mizusawa, Taneyoshi Nakano, Raymond Nosaka,
Tokuji Ono, Tadao Hodai, Seiji Tanigawa,
Yasuo Takata, Robert Takashige,
Billy Takaezu, Seiei Okuma,
Patrick Tokushima, Takeshi Tanaka,
Mack Yazawa, and Yukio Yokota.

And to
Lieutenant Rocco Marzano, Lieutenant Ernest Tanaka,
and Major James Lovell, who were also
part of this mission.

With a special *mahalo nui loa* to Raymond Nosaka,
Tokuji Ono, Diane Ono, Glenna Rhodes, Chika Koida,
Dennis Lehr, and my most enjoyable Cat Island guides,
Barry Foster and Ted Riemann.

I DO SOLEMNLY SWEAR

THAT I WILL SUPPORT AND DEFEND

THE CONSTITUTION OF THE UNITED

STATES AGAINST ALL ENEMIES, FOREIGN

AND DOMESTIC; THAT I WILL BEAR TRUE

FAITH AND ALLEGIANCE TO THE SAME;

AND THAT I WILL OBEY THE ORDERS OF

THE PRESIDENT OF THE UNITED STATES

AND THE ORDERS OF THE OFFICERS

APPOINTED OVER ME, ACCORDING TO

REGULATIONS AND THE UNIFORM CODE

OF MILITARY JUSTICE. SO HELP ME GOD.

—U.S. ARMY OATH OF ENLISTMENT

1

HONOLULU, AUGUST 1941 THE SPIRIT OF JAPAN

I'd be lying if I said I wasn't afraid.

"Bad, bad times," Pop mumbled just yesterday, scowling to himself in the boatyard while reading the Japanese newspaper, *Hawaii Hochi*. He mashed his lips together and tossed the paper into the trash.

I pulled it out when he wasn't looking.

Some haole businessmen were saying all Japanese in Hawaii should be confined to the island of Molokai. Those white guys thought there were too many of us now; we were becoming too powerful. The tension outside Japanese camp in Honolulu was so tight you could almost hear it snapping in the air.

And to make things worse, Japan, Pop's homeland, was stirring up big trouble.

In 1931, when I was six, the Japanese invaded

Manchuria, and they had been pushing deeper into China ever since. Less than a year ago, they'd signed up with Germany and Italy to form the Axis, all of them looking for more land, more power. Then, just last month, Japan flooded into Cambodia and Thailand.

And *my* homeland, the U.S.A., was getting angry.

President Roosevelt was negotiating with Japan to stop its invasions and get out of China, but nothing seemed to be working.

And for every American of Japanese ancestry, Pop was right—these were bad, bad times.

✢ ✢ ✢

That summer I'd just turned sixteen.

Me and my younger brother, Herbie, who was thirteen, helped Pop build boats in his boatyard, a business he'd had since he and Ma came to Hawaii from Hiroshima in 1921. Pop had been making sampan-style fishing boats all his life. He had a skilled apprentice named Bunichi, fresh off the boat from Japan by two years. With all of us helping out, Pop's business managed to survive.

We were finishing up a new forty-footer for a haole from Kaneohe, the first boat Pop had ever made for a white guy. And there would be more, because Pop's reputation had grown beyond Japanese camp. Without question, there was no better boatbuilder in these islands than Koji Okubo, my pop.

We'd been working on this one for more than seven months now, ten hours a day, six days a week.

I was painting the hull bright white over primed wood soaked in boiled linseed oil. I had to strain the paint through fine netting so it would go on like silk, leaving no room for the smallest mistake. Pop lived in the Japanese way of *dame oshi*, which meant everything had to be perfect.

The paint fumes were getting to me, so I climbed down off the ladder to go out back for some fresh air.

A small, flea-infested mutt got up and followed me into the sun. I'd found him a couple of months ago licking oil off old engine parts in the boatyard, and I'd given him some of my lunch. Now that ratty dog stuck to me like glue. I called him Sharky because he growled and showed teeth to everyone but me. Pop didn't like him, but he let him live at the shop to chase away nighttime prowlers.

Pop's shop was right on the water, and just as I walked outside, a Japanese destroyer was heading out of Honolulu Harbor, passing by so close I could hit it with a slingshot. A long line of motionless and orderly guys in white uniforms stood on deck gazing back at the island.

I squinted, studying them as Sharky settled by my feet. Pop suddenly ghosted up next to me, wiping his hands on a paint rag. I could see him in the corner of my eye.

He was forty-eight years old and starting to get a bouncy stomach. A couple inches shorter than me, about five three. His undershirt was white and clean, tucked into khaki pants that hung on him like drying laundry, bunched at his waist with a piece of rope. He had short gray hair that prickled up on his tan head. As usual, he was scowling.

Sharky got up and moved away.

Pop pointed his chin toward the destroyer. "That's

something, ah?" he said in Japanese. "Look at all those fine young men."

They looked proud, all right.

"To them," Pop went on, unusually talkative, "the Emperor is like a god. They would be grateful to die for him."

Grateful to *die*?

Pop's eyes brightened. "The spirit of Satsuma," he said. "That's what lives in those boys—the unbeatable fighting spirit of Satsuma."

He nodded in admiration, then continued on over to the lumber pile to look for something.

What Pop said gave me the willies, because he wanted me and Herbie to be just like those navy guys, all full up with the national spirit of Japan, *Yamato Damashii*. Pop kept a cigar box of cash savings hidden somewhere in the house, money to send us back to Tokyo or Hiroshima to learn about our heritage. "You are *Japanese*," he would say. "How can you learn about your culture and tradition if you don't go to Japan?"

Sure, but what if I got there and war came because the U.S. and Japan couldn't work things out? What if I got trapped and dragged into the Japanese army—or navy, like those guys on that ship? What would I do then? Because I sure didn't feel that kind of spirit. I wasn't a *Japan* Japanese.

I was an American.

Pop's newspaper had said that people around Honolulu were worried they had a "Japanese problem" on their hands—us. What would Japanese Americans do if Japan and the U.S. went to war? Where would our loyalties lie?

4

It was ridiculous, because there was nothing to worry about.

Sure, *issei,* first-generation immigrants like Ma and Pop, were still Japanese citizens. And they lived like they were in Japan, because Japan was inside them too deep. It was hard for them to change their ways.

But I was *nisei,* born and raised here. Ma and Pop gave me and Herbie American names, and we were U.S. citizens. So were my two best friends, Chik and Cobra, who'd just been drafted into the U.S. Army. We were all as loyal to the U.S.A. as anyone else.

"I don't want to go to Japan," Herbie'd whispered to me a couple of months back. "I like it here."

"Yeah, me too," I said.

Like Herbie, I had different dreams from Pop. American dreams. And so did Chik and Cobra.

I watched the Japanese destroyer slip out of sight.

2
CHIK AND
COBRA

Later that day Chik and Cobra showed up at the shop in their snappy new uniforms, home on their first weekend pass.

They were both older than me, just drafted at eighteen, and that was a problem—because now they were at boot camp up at Schofield Barracks on the west end of the island. I was so lost without them I was thinking about signing up.

Chik's real name was Nick Matsumaru, and Cobra's was Takeo Uehara. Their pops worked for Tuna Packers, and our fathers were longtime friends. We were all dock dogs, and had been for as far back as I could remember.

When those two jokers walked into the shop, I was back on the ladder painting the boat. Bunichi was working on the transom lettering, and Pop and Herbie were outside cleaning brushes.

I almost didn't recognize them. Never had I seen them so cleaned up.

"Little man," Cobra called up to me. "You look goofy with your mouth hanging open like that. You never saw army guys this close, or what?"

"You punks!"

"Hey, Bunichi," Cobra called. "Howzit?"

Bunichi waved, then went back to work. His English was terrible, so he didn't talk much unless it was in Japanese, and our Japanese wasn't very good, not like Ma and Pop's.

I covered the paint can and climbed down. Sharky got up and hunched away, showing teeth.

"How you can keep that rat around this place?" Cobra said. "You should put it out of its misery."

"He likes me."

Chik said, "If I ever get that ugly, somebody shoot me, ah?"

"Okay, wait," Cobra said. "Let me get my gun."

"*Ete,*" Chik said.

Cobra shoved him.

"You bazooks," I said, shaking their grips of steel. All our life we'd been together in Japanese camp. That's what we called our part of Kaka'ako, our neighborhood in Honolulu—a camp. We all stuck together by our races. We had Hawaiian camp, Japanese camp, Portuguese camp down by Waikiki, and some Chinese and Filipino.

"So tell me about boot camp," I said.

Cobra shrugged. "Not so bad—if you don't mind sweat and dirt and somebody screaming in your face."

Chik took off his garrison cap and folded it over his belt.

"Ahh!" I said, pointing to his bolohead. "You no more hair! Hoo, your girlfriends not going like that."

"Are you kidding? They love it. They rub my head like it's a bowling ball and kiss my pretty face."

"Pfff," Cobra spat.

Just then, Herbie came in with clean brushes. "Hey," he said, trying not to smile. But he liked those uniforms, too.

Cobra slugged Herbie's shoulder lightly. "How's it going, boss? You like making boats with your pops?"

"Naah. Too hard."

"Rather play baseball, ah?"

Herbie grinned.

"Work hard at that, then," Cobra said. "I know you play good."

"Do my best," Herbie said. "I gotta go. Pop's waiting."

Herbie handed me the brushes and went back outside. I set them on the ladder.

"So really," I said. "Tell me about the army."

Cobra humphed. "We live in tents. Place look like a small city. We call it Boom Town."

"I don't mind it," Chik said. "Of course, I rather be here by the ocean. But when your country calls, gotta go, ah?"

I imagined that city of tents lined up sharp and perfect, guys marching around in snappy uniforms with rifles on their shoulders, shouting, "Hut! Hut! Hut!"

"Ho! Must be great."

I glanced around to make sure Pop was still outside. "Listen," I whispered. "I been thinking I going sign up."

"What! Are you nuts?" Chik said. "You get drafted, sure, but nobody *signs* up."

Cobra snickered and said, "You too young. They not going take you."

"I graduated early, remember? I can show them my high school diploma."

"Won't work."

"Okay, I had ROTC at McKinley—how about that?"

Chik and Cobra looked at each other and broke out laughing, staggering around, holding their sides. *"Rotsie?"* Chik said. "Are you serious? All they do is march around and oil up old rifles with no firing pins."

"So?"

"So boot camp ain't nothing like Rotsie."

"Fine, but look." I checked again for Pop, then pulled my folded-up birth certificate out of my back pocket. I'd brought it along to show them when they stopped by.

Chik grabbed it and squinted.

"If somebody comes, hide it," I whispered.

"Ho, man," Chik said. "This might be a crime."

He handed it to Cobra, who looked it over with raised eyebrows. "You definitely a crazy man," he said. "But it looks pretty good."

I'd used some drawing skills I learned in drafting class to change 1925, the year I was born, to 1923. It was smudgy, but I'd roughed up the whole certificate so that everything looked smudgy.

Cobra rapped his knuckles on my head. "Eddy? Hey. Anybody home in there? Whatchoo doing? You enlist, your

pops going march you right back and tell them you under-
age, ah?"

"No he won't. He's too proud to say anything to anyone
but me."

Chik grinned. "Can I have first crack at your junks after
he shoots you?"

I shoved him.

"Listen," Cobra said. "For real—the army ain't that
much fun. You think it is when you first see it, but it ain't.
Promise."

I shrugged. "I can take it."

Just then Pop came back in with more paint. Cobra
quickly folded the certificate and stuck it in his pocket.

Pop set the bucket down by the ladder and squinted at
their uniforms. "Humph."

Jeese.

Chik winked at me.

My friends didn't mind Pop's grumpy ways. But me and
him were always knocking heads over something. Herbie
was smarter. Kept to himself, just did whatever Pop said and
didn't complain. No *way* I could do that.

"Good to see you again, Mr. Okubo," Cobra said. "How's
business holding up?"

Pop frowned, probably considering if that was a respect-
ful question from someone who'd always been a kid to him.
But Cobra was eighteen now, a man. So Pop tossed him a
crumb. " 'S okay."

Cobra nodded. "Nobody giving you hard time?"

"Why you say that?"

"Fishing. Up at Schofield some guys saying the Hawaiians no like Japanese now, because we got too many sampans. Taking all the fish."

"Unnh," Pop said. "Maybe so, but who you t'ink they come to when they got a bus'up boat?"

Cobra laughed. "Yeah, I guess that would be you."

Pop mumbled something and headed around to the transom, where Bunichi was lettering *Red Hibiscus, Kaneohe*.

Cobra stuck my birth certificate in my shirt pocket. "Forget this, Eddy. Only get you in trouble."

When he and Chik left, I felt all those good times we used to have follow them out. I saluted them silently and picked up my paintbrush.

❖ ❖ ❖

Three weeks later the *Red Hibiscus* was finished—a sleek, sharp-nosed sampan, bright white in the sun. It took ten men and eight mules to hoist and cart her down to the rails and launch her sideways into the harbor, where she sat like a queen on the still water.

Another Okubo masterpiece.

Even Chik and Cobra came down from Schofield to see the launch, because when Pop got paid he'd invite everyone over for Japanese wine, good food, and checkers, like always. A celebration, because by payday we were usually so broke Ma was frying up weeds.

❖ ❖ ❖

Early the next day, me, Herbie, and Pop took the boat for a test run out past Diamond Head. She rode smooth and easy, her knifelike bow slicing the water clean as a shark's fin.

We listened to her sounds, felt her move, saw how she handled in the swells and chop of Kaiwi Channel—and by the time we returned to Kewalo, Pop's usual scowl was long gone.

Herbie dropped the new iron anchor off the bow. We would let the sampan sleep in the harbor overnight. In the morning the new owner would take charge.

I glanced back as we headed home.

Red Hibiscus.

It even had a nice name.

3
RED HIBISCUS

That night Cobra woke me at midnight, banging on the screen door. I stumbled out. "Quiet down," I said. "You going wake everybody up."

He was breathing hard. "You gotta come . . . *now* . . . your boat is burning!"

"What!"

Ma appeared behind me. "What is it, Eddy? Trouble?"

"Pop's boat is on fire."

Ma's hand flew to her mouth.

I ran to wake Pop, then Herbie.

Ma held the screen door open, standing out of the way as the three of us burst past and raced with Cobra down to the harbor, where the *Red Hibiscus* buckled in flames.

We broke through the small crowd gathered on the pier. The orange fireglow flickered on the black water and glowed on grim faces. Chik was there, with his dad and Mr. Uehara, Cobra's dad.

Pop pressed his lips tight.

Mr. Matsumaru was the first to speak. "Somebody said they heard an explosion. Before we got here the fire was already big."

Pop nodded but said nothing.

The blaze shot sharp shadows into the deep sunburned creases around his eyes. He stood watching in his undershirt and wrinkled khaki pants, wearing his grass slippers, too hurried to step into his work boots. The muscles in his jaw rippled under the skin.

I turned away from the fire, sick—all Pop's efforts, all our long days and nights at the shop. The beautiful *Red Hibiscus*—in flames.

How could this be happening?

"I'm sorry, Pop," I said softly.

He didn't respond.

Cobra sat on his heels, looking at a salty stain on the pier. Chik watched the fire, shaking his head.

"Bad, bad, bad," Mr. Matsumaru said.

It was the second mysterious boat burning in less than a year. The first one was a sixty-foot Japanese tuna fisher.

A fireboat came racing in from Honolulu Harbor, but it didn't look like there was much left to save.

"Pop built that boat for a guy from Kaneohe," I said, moving closer to Chik and Cobra. "He was going to pick it up tomorrow."

"Tst," Cobra said, shaking his head.

14

Herbie squatted and crossed his arms over his knees, his scowling face telling me he was as suspicious as I was, because boats don't just explode like that. The last one, somebody poured gasoline on the deck and lit it. Nobody was ever caught.

I leaned forward and peeked around Chik. "Maybe we can save the engine, Pop," I said, remembering how we'd waited weeks for it to be shipped over from the West Coast.

Pop didn't answer, but his friends mumbled how sorry they were as they watched the flames eat up just about every penny we had. Still Pop gave no hint of how he felt.

I squatted next to Herbie. After the fire was out, we'd save what we could and start over. No question. If Pop had agreed to build the haole a boat, then he'd build him a boat—even if he had to borrow money to do it. Pop wouldn't even think about letting a promise or a debt go unpaid.

Somehow, he'd find a way.

But how'd it catch fire? It was too hard to believe it was an accident, like somebody leaving oily rags on board. We were too careful for that.

I tried to think, but my mind was shaken. Twenty years Pop had worked here. *Twenty*. And nobody had ever bothered him. Now this.

All I could do was go back to the Japanese problem, like maybe this was something about Japan and China, and too many Japanese in Hawaii, and people not trusting us, wondering if we would turn on them if the U.S.A. went to war with Japan.

Then also it could have been about angry Hawaiian

fishermen. Or maybe it was because of fear left over from sugar strikes, when so many Japanese workers had taken a stand against the sugarcane growers.

Could have been a lot of things.

When you got two Japanese boats burned up inside of a year, with no explanation, then you got to think the worst.

Nobody spoke, all of us still as stones, watching the flames as the fireboat swept in with water flying like wings from its pumps. But the explosion must have popped a hole in the hull, because the beautiful *Red Hibiscus* went down.

Poof! Gone.

The flames snapped out like a match in a hurricane.

4
SALVAGE

The next morning Chik and Cobra were sitting on our steps waiting to go with me down to the harbor to help with whatever they could. I was lucky to have friends like them.

Pop and Herbie were waiting for us at the pier. The sun was just climbing into a pink morning sky. Out to sea, the ocean breathed slow and soft, a body sleeping under silk.

Herbie sat squatting on his heels. Barefoot, shorts with no shirt, ready to go down and pry parts off the sunken boat.

If Pop suspected somebody of blowing up the boat on purpose, he didn't show it. Thinking about it made my head hot, but he was a rock. When he had problems he couldn't control, he just shrugged and said *Shikataganai*—which meant, pretty much, It can't be helped, why cry over spilled milk? What can you do?

Pop, listen, I wanted to shout. If somebody does

something bad to you, you got to do something about it. You can't just say, That's okay, burn my boat, because that ain't right. Sometimes I just wanted to shake him.

After we lowered two rafts into the water, we tied them off and went back to Pop's shop for two hand-crank winches. We hauled them to the pier in a wagon.

"Where you want these, Pop?" I said.

"Put one on top each raf'," he said. "Then come wit' me. Herbie, you swim out and see what's lef' of that boat, and how deep we gotta go."

Herbie nodded, stood, stretched, and dove in.

Me, Chik, and Cobra followed Pop back to his shop. He dug up two pairs of bamboo goggles and tossed them to Chik. Pop got a hammer, nails, and some old two-by-fours, and we headed back to the harbor, where Herbie waited, dripping seawater.

"What you going do with these woods?" I asked, dropping the two-by-fours on the pier.

Pop answered with a lift of his chin toward the rafts, meaning, You see soon enough.

Fine.

"How deep, Herbie?" Pop said.

"Twenty feet, about."

"Anyt'ing lef' of it?"

"Yeah. We can save some of it."

Pop nodded.

We nailed the two rafts together with the two-by-fours, leaving about five feet of open space between them. We could use the winches to pull up heavy parts through the gap. Not a bad idea.

18

Using small pieces of lumber as paddles, we made our way out into the harbor. I could feel the sun roasting my bare back. Almost all the fishing boats were out. The harbor was quiet.

Cobra's muscles rippled in his back as he pulled water. He was built like a giant tuna, strong and powerful. Calm on the outside, but always on the edge of something on the inside. A typhoon trapped in a tin can. Struck like a snake when he got mad—which is why we called him Cobra.

Chik was the opposite. Kind of bony, always antsy. All the time looking around, tapping on his leg like a drummer, nodding to music nobody else could hear. If you walked close enough to him you could almost feel the beat. Before the army cut it off, his hair was jet-black and combed with sweet-smelling Vaseline hair oil. He liked to puff up and walk around in his fancy silk flowered shirts. And he usually had two or three girlfriends going at the same time; right now he had Fumi, who he'd been chasing around since fifth grade, and a new one, Helen. How he did that without getting caught, I didn't even want to know. Me and Cobra called him Chickaboom—party boy.

At first they called me Babyface, but I said, Cut it out, because I grew up in Kaka'ako and toughed it out at McKinley High just like they did.

Those guys—what would I do if I didn't get into the army with them?

The sampan's dark form wobbled below the raft. Herbie tied a rope around a stone anchor and rolled it into the water. We watched it tumble down and poof on the sand when it hit.

"Let's go take a look," Cobra said.

All of us except Pop slipped off the rafts. Herbie and Cobra got the goggles first. Later, when Chik and me had burning red eyes, we would trade off.

Warm water rushed in around me, the pressure stronger the deeper I went.

The sampan was charcoal black where it had burned. Made me sick to see my nice paint job bubbled and ruined. But we could save the prop, the rudder, the wheel, and most of the hardware.

I studied the hull, gliding in close and running my fingers over it. Just as I'd thought, the explosion had popped a hole in it, right by the fuel tank. Inside, I could see steel gaping like sharks' teeth, and the snapped iron straps that had held the tank in its chocks.

Very suspicious.

When we came back up I told Pop about the hole in the hull. He rubbed the back of his neck, probably wondering how the fuel tank could blow on its own.

"We save what we can," he said. "Bombye we try go get some dry-dock guys to help us bring up the res' of it with a crane."

He worked us like dogs long into the night. Chik and Cobra never complained as Pop cracked the whip. Seemed like old folks like him could only think of work, work, work! You start something, you finish it.

At eleven o'clock he mercifully raised his hand. " 'Nuff for now. Tomorrow we come back."

"About time," I mumbled.

We sank down into the water, then slowly came back up. Cobra grinned at me, water streaming from his face. Chik yawned and shook his head. They knew my pop and his stubborn ways. Herbie was falling asleep, his eyes at half-mast.

But Pop could go all night.

If I ever got into trouble, that old goat would be the first one I'd want at my side.

I nodded thanks and goodbye to Chik and Cobra when we passed by their houses. They didn't have to help us out like that. But that's the way it was with us.

5
SIGNING UP

One morning six weeks later I went downtown.

It was raining, the sky gray.

I was calm.

And it was time.

It was just something I had to do. Especially after we lost that boat. We were Americans, not a "Japanese problem," and if I had to go behind Pop's back and join the army to prove it, then that was what I would do. Sure, I wanted to be with Chik and Cobra. But now it was more than that. Now it was about standing up for something. Pop would be proud of what I was doing, someday.

Also, we needed the money. I would get paid just like Chik and Cobra, and I could give it to Ma. Ever since the boat burned, she'd been so quiet I could tell she was worried. She hardly ate anything, and she had lines on her face that weren't there before. With me making army pay, it would be different.

Even though Chik and Cobra tried to talk me out of it, they vowed to come down from Schofield and watch me lie about my age. They thought it would be funny. "You dreaming," Cobra said on the phone. "They going kick you out so fast your head going spin."

✢ ✢ ✢

They were waiting for me, hunched under a tree just outside the recruitment center, trying to stay dry. I crowded in next to them. "Hey, baboozes, how long you been here?"

"Little bit," Chik said. "Got the early bus."

I took a deep breath, rubbed my hands together. "Let's do it."

"Last chance to forget this," Cobra said.

"Yeah," Chik added. "Don't be crazy."

"I made up my mind."

Cobra threw up his hands. "We tried, ah?"

I headed toward the door.

"The guy going say, Go home, kid," Chik said. "You watch."

But the recruitment officer barely glanced at my birth certificate. Just as he handed me the papers and pen, rain came smacking down so hard I could barely hear him say "Sign here, son."

I wrote: *Eddy Okubo*.

Thunder rolled across Honolulu, and the rain moved out to sea.

"Good luck, soldier," the recruiter said, handing me a copy of the form I'd signed. I stuck it in my back pocket with my folded-up birth certificate.

"Thanks," I said, shaking his hand.

We walked out, me with a new bounce in my step.

"You don't know what you just did," Cobra said.

Who cared? I said I was eighteen and the guy believed it! And now I was in the army with Chik and Cobra.

The sun peeked out bright and steam smoked off the streets. Inland, fresh white clouds grew up out of the mountaintops.

"Ho, do I feel good," I said.

"Go back," Chik said, stopping. "Go back and say, Oops, sorry, I made a mistake, tear up that paper."

Cobra snorted. "Too late. They got him now."

I put my arms around their shoulders. "Looks like you two goofballs stuck with me little bit longer, ah?"

They laughed and shoved me as we headed home, just like we were back in seventh grade.

"What your pops said about it?" Chik asked.

"Said about what?"

"Joining up."

"I didn't tell him."

"What! Ho, man, you *really* crazy." He hunched his shoulders and cringed.

Inside, I cringed, too, because Pop's idea of sending me to Japan for college was shot. He was going to explode.

Or clam up.

You never knew with him, because he lived his whole life inside his head. Ma always said, "Just let him alone, Eddy, let him be. Your daddy's a silent man."

I jammed my hands into my pockets.

Chik kicked a crushed cigarette pack on the road. "Listen, don't tell the army you had Rotsie, or they might make you a lieutenant."

"What's wrong with that?"

"Come on, punk. You too smart. You ain't going be no lifer. Anyone who can graduate high school when he barely sixteen going college someday."

I shrugged. Sure, but I had to get some money first. And besides, it was too late. Like Cobra said—the army got me now.

Cobra patted my head. "You better get a football helmet because your pops going rap your skull with a stick. He might even kill you."

"Kill you twice," Chik said.

Probably. But what could you expect from an old man who refused to even try to understand the American way of life? We just lived in different worlds, me and him. That's all. I liked my island. I had my friends. I had the ocean. I could work and go fishing and live like a king with a couple bucks in my pocket. Japan was part of me, sure. But *this* was my country.

Problem was, I could never figure out how to explain that to Pop. Maybe I could—

No, no, no, don't think about that right now. Think about the sun on your back, breathe some clean air. Soak it up. Feel good for a while.

But it was hard, because I was getting closer and closer to my house.

6
CRANKY
OLD GOAT

Pop was raking leaves under the avocado tree when we reached the small dirt patch we called a yard. Chik and Cobra kept on going, walking backwards, grinning like the cowards they were around him—and around their own pops, too, for that matter.

Pop glanced up when I came through the gate.

He stopped and squinted at me, shadows from the tree spattered all over him. His thin eyelids sagged down at the ends, making me feel like I was being watched by a lizard.

I nodded, then glanced at the house. Maybe Ma would come out to rescue me.

I scratched my cheek, trying to think.

Stupid . . . not to have a plan.

I turned back to Pop and lifted my chin, Hey.

He didn't blink. Dark, hooded eyes.

I looked away.

Opah, a small black and white mixed-breed mutt, came stretching out from under the house. I squatted to pet him.

Think, think.

Opah yawned, his eyes squeezing to slits, his breath like rotting fish.

Pop started raking again.

I stood up.

"Pop," I said, smiling, trying to look cheerful. But I didn't know what was supposed to come after that. "Uh . . . the yard looks nice."

Dumb.

Pop leaned on the rake. Now that sour look said, You got something to say, say it, and stop bothering me.

Okay, I thought. Just get it out, one time fast.

"Pop, I joined the army today," I said. "I was prob'ly going get drafted, anyway . . . you know, like Nick and Takeo? I thought, you know, I might as well get it over with . . . and . . . and . . ."

This part wasn't very clear to me yet.

"Well . . . somebody's got to stand up against the guys who burn sampans because they think we going . . . we . . . I don't know what they think, but it ain't right, you know? So I . . . I . . . I'll send you all my pay, and . . ."

That was all I could think of.

Pop's eyes darted back and forth, and I knew he was translating. I could have made it easier for him and said it in Japanese, but my English was better.

He turned his head slightly, as if listening to a faraway sound. But his eyes didn't move, studying me for way too long.

"Pop?"

He sucked his teeth, then went back to raking leaves.

And that was the end of it. Pop wouldn't look up again. Even if the avocado tree came crashing down, he would just keep on raking.

Opah glanced up at me, like What's going on?

I shook my head and started up the steps to the house. Funny how that old goat gets to me, I thought, because my hands were trembling.

What he was thinking, I could only guess.

Probably he was seeing all those years of Japanese school, all those Boy's Day celebrations with the Japanese red fish flag flying over our house, all the times we'd invited guests from Japan over for dinner so he could talk about his home and tell them how his sons were going to Waseda University—he was probably thinking about all of that— wasted. To him, my joining the U.S. Army was the worst possible betrayal. That was what was banging around in his head. Probably.

I kicked off my rubber slippers and went inside, letting the screen door slap behind me. I winced when I glanced at the flag of Japan nailed to the wall, and the picture of stiff-faced Emperor Hirohito in a frame on the table by our sagging brown couch. If the haoles ever saw that, they would really think they had a Japanese problem. The Emperor's eyes followed me as I crossed the room. Spooky.

Ma was in the kitchen, small and round, black hair turning to gray tied in a knot behind her head.

She smiled, glad to see me home.

"Ma," I said. "I . . . I joined the army today. I was going get drafted anyway, so I . . ."

She gasped and stepped back to fall into a chair. She stared at me a second, my words sinking in, her eyes welling with tears.

I dropped down on one knee and grabbed her hand. "Ma, it's the right thing, specially now when people starting to worry about us because of what Japan is doing in . . . in . . . in China."

A tear slipped from her eye and rolled down her cheek, falling on my hand. "Your *father*, Eddy . . . he . . ."

"I know, Ma, I know."

She rocked, taking her hand back and folding her arms across her chest, leaning into them. "Oh, this is so bad. He has such *dreams* for you. How can you do this to him, Eddy? For so long he has—"

"Do you think I dream those same dreams of his? You know I don't. I have to live my own life. . . . I have to . . . to . . ."

What?

What do I *have* to do that is so hurtful to my family? How come I didn't think of that?

"Look, Ma . . . I'll get paid thirty dollars a month, just like Chik and Cobra. We need the money, don't we? Right?"

She turned away.

"Ma, try to understand."

"Your father knows what's best for you, Eddy. You must respect his wishes. He has taught you better than this."

That was true.

"I'm sorry, Ma."

There was nothing more to say.

Later, when I told Herbie, he stuck to me like a tick, wanting to know if I'd get a gun, or drive a truck or a jeep or a tank. "Can you get me a canteen? One of those ones you hang on the web belt? Ho, man, the army! How come Pop let you do that? You're not even old enough."

"He didn't."

Herbie gaped.

I laughed. A sad laugh.

Because on that day Pop stopped speaking to me. As far as he was concerned, I no longer existed.

7
SKY FIGHTERS

It was a black time, those days before I reported to Schofield. Working in silence at the boat shop was the worst, long stretches broken up only when Bunichi or Herbie said something to me.

Sometimes I dragged around feeling terrible for what I'd done to Pop. Even Sharky could tell something was off. He mostly kept out of sight. Dogs know, somehow.

Other days, I told myself, Listen, it's *your* life, not his. . . . You gotta do what you think is right. If you don't, then you're just his shadow. And serving your country is right.

I tried to think . . . How can I please my family, and honor them—when at the same time I have something to prove?

And then I thought, Pop needs help at work—I got to be there for him. Without me, how will he get by?

✛ ✛ ✛

I passed my physical exam and was inducted into the U.S. Army on October 15, 1941. My new home was a two-man tent down in the lower quadrant of Schofield Barracks.

Boom Town, the city of tents.

I shared mine with a small guy named PeeWee Okazaki, a kid from Maui who played poker like a professional. He could make cards disappear in his hands like magic. Other guys I met were just as full of surprises. There was Shig, full of opinions; and Golden Boy, a dimple-faced ladies' man from Kauai. Another guy, Slim, was over six feet tall. Made the rest of us look like shrimps.

All together there were six hundred of us new island recruits living in those tents with mud trails like roads winding between them—Hawaiian, Chinese, Japanese, lots of races.

Down in Boom Town we didn't have phones or drinking fountains or regular latrines like the mainland guys up in the barracks, but still, I liked it.

I could take it.

✛ ✛ ✛

Basic training was like swimming with barracudas—you were always on edge; somebody screaming in your face hour after hour, day after day.

"New recruit, repeat the army motto!"

"What?"

"Did I ask you to ask me a question?"

"What question?"

"I don't want to hear *anything* but one of four responses, and those four responses are 'Yes, *sir!*' 'No, *sir!*' 'No excuse, *sir!*' And, 'I do not understand, *sir!*' Do you understand *that,* new recruit?"

"Yes, sir. I understand, sir!"

"Are you *stupid,* new recruit, or just plain dumb?"

"What?"

Grunts, they called us. And that was what grunts had to face. It wasn't so bad if you could laugh about it.

Anyway, I was part of something big now, and was too busy learning army rules to worry about anything else, even the *Red Hibiscus* or the Japanese problem.

✢ ✢ ✢

When I came home on my first pass seven weeks after I'd started basic training, Pop still wouldn't speak to me.

To him, I was a ghost.

Even so, I caught him studying me in my uniform one time, and, ho, did that make him angry, getting caught looking. I laughed. I couldn't help it. He huffed out of the room.

But Ma had accepted what I'd done and wouldn't stop fussing over me. "Oh, you must be starving from all that bad army food." "Oh, you must be so tired from working so hard—here, sleep, take a rest." "Oh, you must be anxious to hear about what's going on—here, read the newspaper."

Ahhh!

On Saturday morning, I left the house before she got up. I grabbed my throw net, woke Herbie, and whistled for

Opah, and the three of us went net fishing down past the Chinese rice fields and water buffaloes, where we saw the sun rise over the mountains as we stood knee-deep in the warm ocean.

Mostly we were quiet. But we talked, too.

"Does Pop ever mention my name, Herbie?"

"No."

"That bad, huh?"

"Worse."

I puffed up my cheeks and let the air out slowly. "In a way I don't blame him."

"You asked for it."

"Yeah, that's true."

We managed to catch three fat *moi,* but we couldn't stay long. Herbie had baseball practice, and baseball to him was like fresh air. He played second base for a pretty good junk-yard team called the Kaka'ako Boys.

Ma fried up the fish that night for dinner. Pop ate in silence, staring only at the food on his plate. He wouldn't talk to me, but at least he ate my fish.

I had a hard time sleeping that night, because I missed goading Pop into talking about this or that—didn't matter what, just trying to make him say a few words.

I'd given it a shot, though.

"Hey, Pop," I'd said, then waited for him to turn my way. He didn't.

I said, "Good fishing down by the rice fields. You should go."

His profile said everything: Are you my son? You're not

my son. My son obeys and honors his father. Are you related to me? You my flesh and blood? No.

Finally, I fell asleep.

❖ ❖ ❖

The next morning Herbie shook me awake with wild eyes. "Eddy, get up, get up! Something going on!"

"What?" I said, jumping up and tripping into my shorts. I dragged a T-shirt over my head and stumbled outside after him.

It was noisy. Real noisy.

The sky was swarming with planes.

Some low, some way up.

More were screaming toward us in squadrons from three directions—one group ripping in from the sea, another dropping down over the Waianae range in the west, and the third zipping in over the pass up by Schofield Barracks and Wheeler Field. Must have been two hundred planes, all coming down on Honolulu.

"Who are they, Eddy? Army, navy, or what?"

I didn't answer, because I couldn't believe it. I knew who they were, but it was impossible. How could they get here from—

A fighter blasted overhead just above the treetops, rattling the tin roofs of Japanese camp.

We ducked.

"Ho!" Herbie shouted.

The roar of engines grew louder. Planes filled the sky.

One after another, swooping down, then rising to loop around and dive again. Right over our heads, like mosquitoes swirling at the edge of a campfire.

All over Japanese camp people ran out into the street, squinting up, shading their eyes. Some stood with their hands covering their mouths. A few stayed inside, peeking out their windows.

Fear prickled on my skin. My tongue tingled with brass needles.

"Look!" Herbie said. "They paint um just like Japanese ones."

The fighters ripped down and raced toward Pearl Harbor, the round red *hinomaru* under their wings: the red sun. The symbol of Japan.

A huge explosion shook the earth, somewhere down past Honolulu Harbor. Then another, and another, and after each blast ugly black smoke boiled up over the rooftops.

I grabbed Herbie and shoved him toward the house.

8
DIE BEFORE SHAME

Pop was at the kitchen table when we ran in. A cup of tea sat steaming in front of him.

Ma was at the stove, stooped over fried eggs and rice. "What's wrong?" she gasped, her hand flying to her chest.

"Can't you hear it?"

She glanced up at the ceiling. "Oh, that's just the military, like always."

A plane flew low overhead, shaking the house. Ma frowned. Opah scurried under the table.

Pop said to Herbie, *"Shinbunwa dokonanda? Kyono shinbunwa doshita?"*

"Forget the paper," I said. "Turn on the *radio*."

He glared straight ahead, arms crossed, the radio only inches away from him.

"Pop, *please*! Turn on the *radio*!"

He sat like a stone.

I tumbled down across from him and snapped it on.

Church music.

I spun the dial.

Pop knocked my hand away. *"Rajio kesunda!"* He turned off the radio.

I turned it on.

Pop slapped his hands on the table, stood, and left the room, knocking his cup over. Tea sped across the tabletop and dripped hot onto my leg.

Herbie tried to tell Ma about the planes, but her eyes were following Pop. Eggs spat in the frying pan under her raised spatula.

"Come on, come on," I whispered, begging the radio to tell me something.

The vibration of low-flying fighters rattled through the tin roof and shook the walls and the floor. I could feel Opah trembling against my foot.

"Ma," I said. "I think Japan is attacking us."

Pop heard that and stormed back into the kitchen. The veins on his forehead popped out like soda straws. *"Nandato?"*

The music on the radio stopped and the announcer came on, breathless. "People ah, ah . . . listen, people, you better be calm, ah, people, people, we are under attack by Japanese planes. . . . This is not what you might think, this is not ma-neuvers . . . this is real. . . ."

Pop's face flushed red and the skin around his eyes wrinkled into a squint.

"Masaka!" he spat.

He paced around the kitchen, filling it up. A muscle just below his right eye began to twitch.

"It's true, Pop," I said. "Go outside. Look at the planes, go!"

His eyes jabbed into mine, saying, What kind of son are you to say Japan would do such a dishonorable thing?

He stalked out, the screen door whapping back.

Ma stood with her mouth open, eggs spitting louder on the stove top.

The announcer said, "A lot of you people might think this is a military maneuver. Understand this: this is no maneuver. This is the real McCoy! We are being attacked by Japan!"

Whomp!—an explosion just down the street, so big it rocked our house.

Ma gasped and stumbled back.

Opah ran out from under the table as another fighter boomed overhead, its engine rattling my teeth. I squatted down and picked him up, his paws raking my chest.

Pop staggered back into the kitchen, his eyes glazed, skin ghostly gray.

Was he hurt? I set Opah down and went to him. But I was afraid to touch him. I never touched him.

There was no blood that I could see, no wound. Just those spooked eyes.

I let my hand fall on his shoulder.

"Pop," I said. He would not have allowed this even five minutes before. But now he didn't bat my hand away.

The announcer said, "All military personnel return to your posts immediately. . . . I repeat, *immediately*! All civilian defense workers report to your jobs. . . . We are under attack. . . . All civilians take cover. . . . Stay indoors. . . . This is no joke. . . . We're being bombed by the Rising Sun! I repeat, all military personnel return to your posts immediately!"

That meant me.

Pop sagged against the wall. I tried to support him, but he waved me off. Herbie stood frozen, eyes darting from me to Pop to Ma.

I ran to my room to get my uniform on.

Ma hurried after me, the spatula still in her hand. She grabbed my shirt. "Eddy . . . don't go—"

"No!" Pop shouted.

Ma yelped and dropped the spatula. She broke into sobs, covering her face with her hands.

"No," Pop said again, this time more softly. "You go, boy. Go back army."

My throat burned at the sound of his voice.

And at the look in his eyes.

Son, they said. Son.

He blinked and looked down at his hands. For his homeland to have attacked us this way—a sneak attack—was warfare of the worst kind. Cowardly and shameful.

I could tell there was more he wanted to say. I could read it all over his face: Eddy, do something. . . . Do something. . . .

Herbie was backed up against the wall, as if trying to seep into it, to hide. I put my hand on his shoulder. "Stay strong," I said. "I need you now."

He stood frozen.

Ma's sobbing made my throat burn worse. I put my arm around her. "It's okay, Ma. We going be all right."

She looked so lost and afraid.

"You go," Pop demanded, his voice raspy. "Go back army. You no can stay. Bad, bad, time now. You solja. . . . You go back barracks." His eyes were stunned.

"No make *haji,* Eddy," he went on, saying my name for the first time I could remember. He usually called me boy. For a second I didn't know who he was talking to.

"Pop—" My voice broke.

"No make shame for this family. You go. Fight for your country. Die, even, but die with honor."

I looked into his eyes, letting him know I understood, that I would honor him, that I would honor us all.

"You come back dead before you shame us."

His eyes were steady.

Neither of us looked away.

✢ ✢ ✢

In my room I ripped off my T-shirt and shorts and stumbled into my uniform. My shiny brown shoes were outside on the porch.

Herbie sat on the bed watching me. I wondered if he had any idea how bad it was that we were being bombed by Japan. It was crazy. They'd just poked a wasp's nest with a stick.

"Herbie, you got to watch Pop. He's in shock or something. He's confused."

Herbie scowled, his eyebrows drawn together.

41

"It's up to you now," I said. "You the man standing next in line to Pop." I put my hand on his shoulder. "Come, walk outside with me."

In the kitchen I hugged Ma goodbye and kissed the top of her head. "I gotta go. Don't—"

She pulled me closer and buried her face in my chest.

"Ma," I said, pushing her back and looking into her eyes. "Don't worry about me. I going be fine, and so will you and Pop and Herbie. I promise." I hugged her again and ran out.

On the porch I stepped into my shoes and tied them quickly. Pop's work boots stood guard next to Ma's grass slippers, like always. I stared at them, choking up.

I wondered if I'd ever see them again.

Maybe not.

Herbie followed me out to the street. Planes sped past overhead, engines screaming, earth shaking, Ma's shadow framed in the screen door.

I reached out to shake Herbie's hand. His grip was stronger than I thought it would be. I pulled him close and hugged him for the first time in my life. I slapped him once on the back, then let go.

"Help Ma, okay? Things going get tough now. You got to be strong. I know you can do it."

Herbie nodded.

We looked at each other. I felt bad putting weight on him like that. But what could I do?

"Strong," I said.

Just down the street, Pop stood with his back swayed, gazing up at a sky smeared with the ugly black bursts of antiaircraft fire. Down toward Pearl Harbor fat black columns of smoke boiled into the clouds.

I wanted Pop to see that I was leaving. I wanted him to say goodbye, to say something, anything. I wanted him to know I wouldn't let him down. I would never shame him, not in a million years.

I mashed my lips together, then turned and headed downtown.

9
CHAOS

Honolulu was a mess.

Cars zipping around, ignoring red lights and stop signs. Police sirens, ambulances, fire engines, horns, people shouting. Now I could hear machine-gun fire mixed in with the rumble of planes. Nothing seemed real. Was the world coming to an end? A bomb could fall on me and—*boom!*—I'm gone.

I headed downtown, looking out for Chik and Cobra, who were also home on pass. I ran by Advertiser Square, the old missionary church, the palace, cutting through yards, crossing soft grass in the shade of monkeypod trees, while all around, uniformed guys like me raced toward the Army-Navy YMCA, where the buses would be.

Amazingly, I spotted Chik running up ahead, his unbuttoned shirt streaming out behind him.

"Chik!" I yelled.

He glanced over his shoulder and stopped.

"Ho, man!" he said. "What *is* all this?"

"You seen Cobra?"

"Not since Friday night."

"Look at all these guys," I said. "How we going get back to Schofield?"

Down near Pearl Harbor more and more black smoke was piling into the sky, rising up darker and dirtier and uglier by the second.

Chik said, "Man, I was only home for half an hour before all this noise. What a party last night. How come I never saw you at Jiro's place?"

"*Party?* How can you even *think* about that now?"

Before he could answer, a thundering explosion rocked the street just blocks away. We covered our heads and ducked, then looked at each other and took off running.

We ran past bars and cafés and arcades and tattoo parlors, the streets tangled with military and emergency vehicles and guys trying to hitch rides back to their posts.

But there were way too many of them.

"Chik! Eddy!" We turned and saw Cobra shoving his way toward us.

"Hey," Chik said, his white teeth flashing. "How come you never showed up at Jiro's party? I thought for sure you—"

"Are you *nuts*?" Cobra said. "Talking about—"

He stopped and looked up.

The skies had fallen eerily silent. Between the buildings that ran down to Honolulu Harbor we could see the planes

45

racing away, little specks regrouping and zipping out to sea. I checked my watch. Eight-forty.

"It's over," I whispered.

"For those guys it is," Cobra said. "They gotta be running low on fuel. Must be a carrier out there." He slapped my shoulder. "We got to find us a bus."

"Wait—I have an idea," I said, and took off up the street, away from the crowds. A bus, if we could even find one, would take too long.

They ran after me, Cobra yelling, "What are you *doing*?"

We needed a car.

A black Packard broke away from the traffic jam and sped toward me. The red-haired haole driver honked—*Blaat! Blatt!*—hunched over the steering wheel.

I waved my hands above my head. "Stop! Stop!"

Blaaaaaaaat!

"Eddy!" Cobra shouted. "Get out of the way!"

The haole slammed on the brakes. The engine stalled, and he fumbled to start it. I could see he was scared. He tried to roll his window up, but I ran over and put some weight on it.

"Get away from me!" the guy shouted.

Chik and Cobra crowded in.

"You don't understand," I shouted. "We gotta get back to Schofield. We're soldiers. We need a ride."

The car sprang back to life.

"Here," I said, ripping my wallet out. "You don't believe the uniform, then check my ID, look!"

The guy glanced at it and frowned.

"We'll pay you," I said. "Here, take all my money." I

yanked out all the bills I had, twenty-two dollars. "Cobra, Chik, give him everything you got!"

The haole grabbed the bills, trying to shove them back out the window. "I can't take this. I have to go."

"Please, mister, we got to get to our *post*. We're at *war*. They need us at Schofield."

He glanced at the smoke rising from Pearl Harbor. "How do I know you're not one of . . . of them?"

"Who?" I said.

He pointed toward the planes out on the horizon. "Them!"

I shoved my ID in his face. "You see where it says *United States* Army?"

The guy jerked his head back. "All right, all right, get in."

We piled into the backseat.

"Where was it you needed to go again?"

"Schofield Barracks."

He frowned. Schofield was thirty-five miles away.

Chik looked like he wanted to strangle the guy. Cobra ducked his head out the window, peeking up at the sky as we raced out of downtown Honolulu.

The haole said, "I'm Jack. Sorry for being suspicious, it's just—"

" 'S okay," Cobra said. "No worry about it."

"Yeah," Chik added. "We all jumpy."

Boy, was that the truth.

When we hit Kam Highway we gasped at the black dragons of smoke snaking up out of Pearl Harbor. Cobra, hanging halfway out the window, shouted, "Hang on, boys, they coming back!"

A new squadron of fighters screamed down over the mountains. And then another swept in behind us, banking low around Diamond Head.

The fighters swooped down in V formation, heading straight toward the fiery devastation.

High above the fighters, bombers crawled across the sky over Pearl Harbor and Hickam Field, each letting loose their belts of steel death. You could see the bombs falling, falling, disappearing into the smoke, then—*Ka-boom!*—buckling and obliterating the helpless parked planes and ships.

We gaped at Pearl Harbor as we sped by just above it. The battleships were being eaten by flames that flicked out like lizard tongues. Some ships were underwater with their superstructures showing. Others leaned against the dock.

"They coming to finish the job," Chik said. "Those ships are sitting ducks."

Traffic came to a halt.

Just ahead a group of SPs, the Navy police, were turning cars back or forcing them off the road.

Fighters raced in overhead, and the SPs scattered into a ditch. When the planes had passed, they crawled back out.

"Come on, come on," I mumbled, pounding my fist on the back of the front seat.

Even up at Schofield, miles away, I could see smoke. Above us, the sky was splattered with black puffs of navy antiaircraft fire.

The SP glanced into our car.

"I gotta get these guys to Schofield," Jack said. We held up our IDs, and the SP waved us through.

Just then, sweeping in from the mountains, a single fighter came down on us with snaps of flame flickering in its gunports. Dusty puffs of red dirt and weeds jumped out of the ground in twin trails racing straight toward us. The SP hit the dirt by the left front tire. Jack gaped at the machine-gun tracks. Cobra and Chik piled over me, all of us diving to the floor and covering our heads with our arms as bullets ripped across the hood—*thwack-thwack-thwack!*

The engine died.

The fighter boomed past and dropped down into Pearl. We inched up and watched it. Jack sat with his eyes frozen wide open.

"Hey," I said, shaking him. "Wake up. Start the car. We gotta get out of here! Wake up!"

Jack shook his head and fumbled with the ignition, his fingers trembling wildly.

Nothing happened.

He tried again, and when the car coughed to life we cheered.

Jack gunned it. The Packard jerked forward, but the engine sounded raspy. "We're never gonna make it," he said.

"We got to," Cobra said.

Something huge blew down in Pearl, so big it whoomped through the car. "Good Lord!" Jack said. "What was *that*?"

A hideous monster of smoke boiled up, red and orange and black, a volcanic fireball climbing into the sky. At its base, huge flames shot out like claws, reaching across to the ships nearby. The whole harbor was burning, even the water.

"God bless their poor souls," Jack said.

I turned away, sick, trying not to think about the blood and pain and agony down there.

Jack got the car moving again, a smoking, slow-moving target for the next fighter that dropped down out of the sky.

10
SCHOFIELD BARRACKS

At Schofield we gave Jack a thumbs-up and sprinted for the gate. Inside, jeeps raced around, swerving, jumping curbs to get past stopped vehicles. Men scurried like roaches, shouting and stacking equipment.

We ran through the quad and headed across the parade grounds to our platoon down in Boom Town.

When I burst into my tent, PeeWee was on his knees packing his equipment.

"Hey!" he said. "You made it!"

"Wasn't easy."

"Check this out," he said, sticking his finger through a bullet hole in the tent right above my cot.

I looked down and saw that there was also a hole in my pillow. "Yah! From the Japanese *planes*?"

"Yep."

"Jeese! I could have been sleeping there!"

"Make up your field pack," PeeWee said. "We're moving out."

"To where?"

"Who knows?"

PeeWee dragged his pack and barracks bag out. I pulled off my suntans and put on my field gear, then packed up.

I found my platoon out on the parade grounds, where everyone was waiting for orders.

Up in the quad, men moved and trucks rumbled. I dropped down next to PeeWee, wondering why they weren't sending any trucks down to get us.

"Who's in charge?" I said.

"Nobody."

Chik came over, then Cobra, Shig, and Golden Boy.

"Hey, Shig," I said. "How you got back?"

"Never went home. Stayed here for all the fun."

"What fun?" Chik said, probably thinking he'd missed a party.

"We got strafed. They shot up the field. You dig in the grass, you going come up with lead. But those planes didn't care about us, no. They wanted those fighters all lined up over by Wheeler Field. All we got was the stray bullets. But we shot one plane down."

"For real?"

"Yeah, this one Zero was coming in so low I could hit it with a rock! I look up and see the pilot and he had on a white scarf, and he was grinning at us—*grinning,* I tell you. So this guy with a Browning came running out in the open and—*bababababababa!*—he start blasting away—bullets flying up at the plane, the guy staggering around trying for hold on to that heavy gun. Pretty soon you see one small smoke coming from the back of the plane. Then the smoke got more big, and more big, and the plane tip to the side. Bugga going down, ah? Spooky, to see that, because right then you know the guy in that plane going die."

"Ho, *man*!" Chik said.

I tried to picture it, but all I knew about war was how to do push-ups, dig foxholes, crawl around in the mud, and clean my Springfield.

PeeWee squinted up at the trucks in the quad. "They not moving very fast up there. Maybe they going send us down to help out at Pearl."

"Naah," Cobra said. "Got to be the beaches, ah? Because what if the Japanese try come ashore? Somebody gotta be there to stop them, and maybe that somebody going be us."

Us?

A picture flashed in my mind: thousands of Japanese soldiers screaming ashore with their silver bayonets gleaming in the moonlight.

❖ ❖ ❖

An hour later, the men up in the quad started making their way onto the trucks.

But we just sat there, silent, watching as truck after truck after truck moved out.

When they were all gone, Schofield fell silent.

And six hundred island boys still sat waiting.

Thirty minutes later a weapons carrier bounced across

the parade grounds. It pulled up and stopped. Two men got out.

The big guy was a lieutenant. He stood tall, his hat at a slight angle.

The driver was smaller, a grunt, like us.

While the grunt lowered the tailgate, the lieutenant studied us with tight, squinty eyes.

"I'm Lieutenant Sweet," he said, then waited, daring someone to mumble something about his name.

He nodded toward the weapons carrier. "What we have here is a truck full of tools. We are going to use these tools to dig trenches across this field, trenches wide enough to jump into. When we're done with that, we'll find other locations to defend."

Dig ditches? I thought, You got the whole Japanese imperial force dropping bombs on us, ready to invade by sea—and you want us to dig ditches?

"Step out of line," Lieutenant Sweet went on, "and we got that nice stockade down yonder just waiting for you. In case you don't know what a stockade is, it's a prison."

I glanced down the way at the white building with its green roof. A chain-link fence ran around it, with gun towers at the corners. The windows were barred.

Lieutenant Sweet grinned when he saw us looking. "We just turned everyone in it loose so each of those good men could go do his fighting. You Japs look cross-eyed at anything but those trenches and you'll be taking up where they left off. Understand what I'm saying here?"

Japs?

"Form a line," he spat.

"Did he say Japs?" I whispered to Cobra.

Cobra squinted, silent.

The grunt driver tossed us picks and shovels.

Lieutenant Sweet barked, "You and you, dig a trench from here to that tree. You men over there, get that pile of burlap sacks out of the truck and fill them with dirt."

"You call me a Jap," I muttered to Chik, "I going laugh and shove you, because you a Jap, too, ah? But when somebody like him says it—"

I spat, then wiped my mouth on my shoulder.

"Shhh," Chik said. "You want him to hear you?"

"Fool think everybody here Japanese," PeeWee said. "Can't even tell Hawaiian from Chinese from Filipino or what."

"Don't matter," Shig said. "He don't trust any of us."

"We second-rate soldiers now?" Cobra said. "Only good for dig holes? Not good enough to fight for our own island?"

"Shut up!" Chik said. "He going *hear* you."

"Look like I care?"

"You heard what he said about that stockade."

Cobra spat.

"They going get this straightened out," Chik said. "You watch."

"They better," I said.

We dug ditches all afternoon.

At five o'clock, Lieutenant Sweet ordered us back to our tents, where we unpacked everything we'd been told to pack.

Soon three heavy trucks rolled down, one with water, the next with huge aluminum pots of stew and applesauce; the third was another weapons carrier. We dragged ourselves up and stood in line with our tin field plates. We ate in silence, then filled our canteens.

Lieutenant Sweet climbed up onto the hood of a truck. "Listen up and listen good. This truck is a weapons carrier. There is a weapon aboard for each of you. You will be given two clips of ammunition. You are to load up, but under no circumstances are you to lever a round into the chamber of your rifle."

Sweet paused, glowering.

"We've had reports of enemy paratroopers landing all over this island, including in these hills above us."

I glanced up at the clouds moving over a darkening sky. If there were paratroopers up in the hills, they'd be hard to find, because the jungle was dense, and when night falls in the islands it falls like a hammer.

A mumble rippled through the platoons.

Lieutenant Sweet grinned. "You grunts are going up there to find them . . . and kill them."

11
JUNGLE PATROL

Lieutenant Sweet paired me up with Cobra.

I was so tired from digging ditches I had to keep slapping my face to stay awake as we started out. But when I thought *paratroopers,* my eyes popped open.

Night fell black as paint. The smell of burning rubber from the fires at Wheeler Field hung faintly in the air. The only sounds were our boots crunching into the bushes. When somebody stepped on a stick, it snapped like a firecracker.

I glanced back. In daylight you could see all the way down to the ocean. But now the island was blacked out. All of it. Not even the smallest dot of light anywhere.

Cobra was right in front of me, but I could hardly see him. "Wait," I whispered, reaching out to touch the back of his field pack.

He stopped with a jolt. "What?"

"If I can't even see you, how we going see a paratrooper?"

"What about our own guys?" he whispered. "We could shoot each other."

"No kidding."

We stumbled on into the darkness.

I could follow Cobra's shape if I stayed close. But if he got too far ahead of me, he was gone.

An hour passed.

We had no idea where we were or how far we'd come. What if the paratroopers were hiding, waiting for us to walk into a trap?

"Cobra," I whispered. "Maybe we should stop and listen."

We huddled close and crouched in the blackness. I bolted a round into my Springfield. "If I hear anything I going yell 'Halt!' " I whispered. "And I better like the answer."

There was a rustling sound. Somebody coming through the ferns, crushing leaves.

We hit the ground, our rifles pointing toward the noise. I hooked my finger around the trigger.

The rustling came closer, closer.

Stopped.

I peeked up, but nothing was there, not even the shape of something. I held my breath.

A few seconds later the rustling started up again. Sweat dripped into my eyes.

I heard a huffing sound. Then a grunt and hollow breathing.

"Halt!" I shouted. "Identify yourself!"

The rustling got louder, turning frantic. My heart leaped, slamming in my throat. This guy sounded *big*. And he wasn't answering. Maybe he was charging us, not stopping, not running away.

Cobra and I shot at the same time.

Bam! Boom!

A moan jarred the night. Then a heavy thump, followed by the sound of escaping air.

I bolted another round into my rifle, my hands shaking so bad I could hardly get my finger back inside the trigger guard.

"I think we got him," Cobra whispered.

"We should wait till morning, when we can see," I said. "He could be playing dead, waiting for us to make a noise so he can find us and shoot us."

Barely breathing, we waited.

Dawn came on slowly, long hours later. My whole body ached from not moving. I squinted into the oily morning light, my mouth dry as chicken feathers.

The jungle turned to shadows, then shapes—trees, vines, ferns.

Pieces of sky.

We peeked up over the weeds at the body.

A cow.

We'd shot a cow.

Cobra groaned. We creaked up and walked over to it with our Springfields crossed over our chests. Its mouth was frozen in a gape, a purple tongue with dirt stuck to it sagging to one side. A dark puddle of blood soaked the earth just below its neck from a single bullet wound.

I felt sick to my stomach.

✢ ✢ ✢

A half hour later we were back down in camp. All around us other soldiers emerged like ghosts out of the trees and bushes.

Lieutenant Sweet sat in a truck, drinking coffee.

I threw down my field pack and took off my boots, keeping quiet about the cow, because Cobra thought we'd never hear the end of that.

Lieutenant Sweet got out of the truck. "All right," he said, hitching up his pants. "Looks like the paratrooper thing was only a rumor. Go back to your tents and eat. The mess truck will be coming down shortly. After that, try to get some sleep. You'll hear from me again at ten hundred hours."

✢ ✢ ✢

Later that morning I stumbled into formation, foggy and confused.

"Remember these?" Lieutenant Sweet said, sweeping his hand toward the tool truck. "Grab something."

We dug trenches.

We carried sandbags.

We strung barbed wire.

After evening chow we staggered back to our tents and fell asleep in our own stink.

12
EYES OF THE EMPEROR

On the afternoon of December 10, Sweet hit us with another bombshell.

"Form up!"

We scrambled into position. "All Japs move over to my right," he said. "The rest of you stay where you are."

I hesitated, stunned again by how ugly that word sounded coming from his mouth.

I glared at Sweet, getting angrier and angrier about how the army was treating us, like we couldn't be trusted. Just Japs. Burn their sampans. Separate them from the real soldiers, the loyal ones.

"Now!" Sweet shouted.

Slowly, I fell in with the rest.

Sweet dismissed the other troops and turned back to us. "Get your rifles and bayonets and bring them and any ammunition you have over to these trucks. The supply sergeant will check them in. Then gather your belongings and take down your shelters and relocate them over there."

He turned and pointed to a weedy patch of red dirt on the other side of the field.

"You are not to leave the immediate vicinity of your shelters for any reason without permission, not even to go to the latrine, is that understood?"

No one answered. Not one man.

"Is that *understood*?"

✛ ✛ ✛

For half the night I listened to men standing just outside the flaps of their tents relieving themselves. Never in all my life had I heard a sound as lonely as that.

✛ ✛ ✛

Reveille woke us at five the next morning.

I stepped out into the warm air . . . and froze.

A sick, sour taste rose in my throat. Because what I saw were eyes.

Eyes behind sandbags.

Eyes behind machine guns.

Eyes all around us.

Other soldiers came out of their tents, yawning and stretching.

Waking to those eyes.

Sweet was leaning against a truck parked just inside the

ring of machine guns. "Rise and shine to a new day, miserable grunts, and listen up. You will each receive a supply of field rations, but you will do no work. You will remain here. When you need to use the latrine, you will ask permission to be escorted to it."

We were under *guard*?

"Please," he said. "Somebody step out of line. Anyone. I would *love* to deal with that."

We got our rations and milled around the tents.

I felt like I'd been stabbed with a broken bottle. What were they thinking? That we were going join up with the guys who bombed us? Were they insane?

It got worse.

Later that day, Chik got a note from his Wahiawa girlfriend, Helen. She said the FBI was going into Japanese homes all over the island, arresting men and taking them away. *Lot of families are so afraid,* she wrote.

It made my head spin.

No, no, no, this is all wrong.

I couldn't stand still. Pacing, pacing. Had they arrested Pop? Or even *Herbie*?

I had to know.

What was going on out there? All we got were rumors and notes slipped inside from families and friends.

That night I asked a guard for permission to call home.

"Can't let you do that," he said. "Orders."

"But— "

"Now you just go on back to your tent before you get yourself in more trouble than you might care to be in, you hear?"

What could I do?

"My cousin," Shig said later that night in our blacked-out bivouac. "You know where he's at? Japan. He went to visit my dad's family. Now he's stuck there."

I cringed; that had been my own fear.

"Ho," Chik said. "What if they make him go in the Japan army?"

Shig's eyes widened. "Ahh! Me and him could come face to face on the battlefield. What I going do then?"

Cobra spat into the darkness. "Ain't going be no battlefield, you fool. Not for you, anyways. You done. You not even a grunt no more. You a prisoner now. The army ain't going say it, but when they look at us they don't see soldiers. What they see is Japs. What they see is enemies."

"Maybe," Chik said. "But they going straighten it out. They just confused now. Nobody knows what to do with us, that's all. Gotta be something like that."

"Pfff."

"What?" Chik said.

"Nothing."

"No, tell me. Whatchoo thinking?"

Cobra spat again. "Okay. Listen. Try see what I saying, ah? First, they split you off from all the other local guys, right? Then they take away your Springfield, your bayonet, your bullets, and your pocketknife, if you was dumb enough to give them that. Then they make you go bat'room in the dirt by your tent, and when you wake up next day you got machine guns all around you. You gotta look at that and think, We prisoners. Right? Am I right, Eddy?"

"You right," I said, scraping mud off my boots with a

64

stick. Who cared anymore? Seemed like we were guilty no matter what we did. So why even fight it? Like Pop always said—*Shikataganai*, Way it is.

But the next day the machine guns were gone.

Nobody ever said a word about why they came or why they left.

⁘ ⁘ ⁘

Then the army stopped training us.

The Hawaiians, Portuguese, and Chinese still got trained. But all the Japanese got was cleanup work, what they gave to the lowest boot camp grunts. Shoeshine boys and dishwashers.

"They so wrong about us, Cobra," I said, hunching over my tin dinner plate. "Makes me mad."

He nodded. "To them we all look like Hirohito. They see us, they see the guys in those planes dropping bombs on them. We got the eyes of the Emperor. They scared of us. Scared."

13
IMMIGRATION

That afternoon we were free to go where we wanted. So I went up to the post exchange, the army store, and stood in line to call home.

We didn't have a telephone at our house, so I had to call the Higashis, our next-door neighbors.

Mrs. Higashi answered on the second ring. *"Moshi-moshi."*

"Mrs. Higashi," I said. "This is Eddy Okubo."

"Eddy!"

"I'm trying to find Ma, or Herbie, if she's not home."

"Oh, oh, yes, you went army, I remember. Wait, I go find your mama."

She clunked the phone down. I could hear her scurrying out.

A minute later Ma came on the line, out of breath. "Eddy . . . is that you?"

"It's me, Ma, is everything okay? Where's Pop, where's Herbie?"

A long pause.

"We all right," she said. "What about you? Are you eating? Do you have enough—"

"Ma, I'm fine, but what about Pop? Is he home?"

That silence again.

"Ma?"

"He went down Immigration, day after those planes came. He . . . he turn himself in."

"*Why*, Ma? What did he do?"

"You know him, so stubborn when he get some idea."

"What idea, Ma?"

"He went down there because he was ashamed for what Japan did. . . . It hurt him, Eddy."

"Where's he now?"

"Nobody knows. He didn't come back yet."

"But that was almost a week ago."

"Lot of men got arrested."

"Where's Herbie?"

"Home. He's okay."

"What about Bunichi? Where's he?"

"I don't know."

"But why would they keep Pop? He didn't do anything. They can't just hold him for . . . for *what*?"

She didn't answer.

"Ma. How you going live? How you going get money?"

"We have savings."

The cigar box. College money. Everything Pop had saved. "Listen, Ma. The army pays me thirty dollars a month, remember? I send you that."

" 'S okay, Eddy. We have friends—the Higashis, the Hamamotos. And Herbie working part-time. They need lot of help down the harbor right now, fixing boats. Don't worry about us. You just stay safe, Eddy."

"Nothing going happen to me, Ma."

I listened to her breathing.

We were running out of things to say. I could hear Mrs. Higashi in the background, calling her cat.

"Ma, if Pop comes home tell him to call Schofield and leave a message, okay? I want to know the minute he gets back, or else I going keep worrying about him. If Pop won't call, tell Herbie. Okay, Ma? Will you do that?"

"I tell Herbie to call you."

"Good. And you call me too if you need something, okay? Anything. I'll get it if I can. You promise to call me?"

She fumbled with the phone, a raspy sound, like she was rubbing her hand over the mouthpiece.

"Ma," I said. "Everything going be fine."

She said nothing.

Then: "You . . . you need me send you something? You need . . ." Her voice trailed off.

I closed my eyes and leaned into the phone booth. Got to be so hard on her—me gone, Pop gone. Lucky Herbie was still there, and lucky he was getting big now, and stronger.

"I have everything I need, Ma."

"Eddy?"

"Yeah?"

"What we going do?"

Words stuck in my throat. Just like they always did for Pop. I should never have joined the army. I should be home.

"Me and Herbie," I said, searching for an answer. "Ma . . . we going find a way to hold everything together if they don't let Pop go. Don't worry. We going come out okay."

There was a long silence.

"Ma?"

Mrs. Higashi came on the phone. "Eddy? I help your mama now. She's overcome. I take care of her, don't you worry, she going be fine."

She hung up.

I stood holding the receiver, then slowly set it on the hook.

14
ORDERS

Three days later, I got a message to call home. I ran up to the PX and dialed the Higashis. When Herbie finally came on the line, the front of my shirt was dark with sweat.

"Ma said to call when we knew about Pop," he said.

"Where is he, Herbie? Is he okay?"

"He's home. The FBI arrested lot of guys—Shinto and Buddhist priests, language-school teachers, even fishermen. But not Pop. They kept him at Immigration for a while, asking questions. They searched his shop, too. But they let him go because they need him for help fix small boats."

"So Pop's all right?"

"Same old grumbly self. Just like Sharky. You should have seen the FBI guys trying to walk around that dog. Was funny."

I took a deep breath and leaned against the phone booth. Pop was home.

"Where's Bunichi, Herbie? Ma didn't know."

"He's around, because they need him, too."

That was a relief.

"Guess what?" Herbie went on. "They had these guards down at Kewalo, and they put one of them on every Japanese boat. They had big iron picks and were supposed to smash a hole in the bottom if they got an order to sink them."

"What?"

"They gone now, the guards. They were there for three days."

"That's crazy," I said.

"That's not all. Some MPs came by our house and searched your room."

"MPs? Like army MPs?"

"Yeah, army. They made a real mess in there. What they were looking for, I don't know, but they didn't find anything or take anything, except our radio."

That made me so mad I couldn't speak! MPs searching my room! When will it end? When I'm in the stockade? When I'm dead?

"Eddy?"

"I'm here, just . . . never mind. What about Chik and Cobra's pops? They get arrested?"

"Naah, they need all those guys for fix boats."

"And Ma, how's she doing?"

"We getting by. Stop worrying and go do army, ah? I'm here."

"Yeah, you there, that's right. Thanks, Herbie. You call again, you got something, okay?"

"Sure."

"It's good to talk to you, you know? Good to hear your voice."

"Yeah."

"Man, Herbie, I . . . listen, just stay safe, ah?"

"You too, Eddy. You too."

✛ ✛ ✛

Later that morning, Sweet drove down to our bivouac in the mess truck. Another officer was with him. When he got closer, I couldn't believe it—it was Mr. Parrish, our mechanical drawing teacher at McKinley High School.

Ho! Mr. Parrish was a captain, two silver bars on his uniform. He was okay, a haole who understood local guys like us. I remembered he said he was in the National Guard. I guess he got called up.

"Things looking better," Chik said. "At least he knows we not spies from Japan, ah?"

Sweet got out and barked, "Atten-*hut!*"

We snapped to attention.

"At ease," Sweet said. "Gather round and sit on the grass. Let's go! Look alive! Get the lead out!

"Now listen up," he said. "The captain has a few words for you."

Captain Parrish studied us. When he spoke, the sound of his voice took me right back to drafting class. "What happened with the machine guns was a mistake," he said.

"That's all I'm at liberty to say about the incident, except that I would personally like to extend an apology."

A few heads nodded.

Cobra sat unmoved.

"Today we'll spend the afternoon on the rifle range," Captain Parrish went on. "Tomorrow you're moving out to the beaches. You'll get your weapons right after midday chow."

Cobra turned to the side and spat.

✤ ✤ ✤

When the sound of taps in the quad ended the day, I lay wrapped in my scratchy army-issue blanket with the tent flap open, looking out at the shadowy clouds gliding over the stars, sails crossing a dark sea.

A perfect time for another attack.

15
LOOK BACK
AND DIE

The next morning we squeezed onto troop trucks and headed out. "Jeese, Chik," I said. "When was the last time you took a shower? You stink."

"*Man* smell, son."

"Pshh."

Golden Boy and PeeWee jabbered like they were going to a football game. Cobra smiled, listening. He closed his eyes and leaned his head back.

But when we drove by Pearl Harbor, with the sad hulls of crushed ships clearly visible, we shut up.

Even now, small snakes of smoke trailed into the sky, like smoldering campfires. It seemed quiet down there, peaceful almost. I could see trucks and jeeps and men moving around, working cranes, maneuvering tugboats, trying to save the hammered destroyers and clean up the mess.

An hour later we convoyed around the end of the island and plunged down into Waimanalo, a narrow corridor of green farmland with towering mountains on the left and a long sand beach on the right.

Shig raised his chin. "If they going attack from the ocean, this is the place. All that sand. Easy."

One by one, the trucks pulled off the road, men scrambling out with their gear. Our truck and three others headed down a side street toward the ocean. Sweet's truck backtracked up a lane that paralleled the beach. "Good riddance," Shig said. "I hope he don't come bothering us."

Cobra snorted. "You dreaming."

We stopped at the end of the road and piled out with our gear, the bright, sunny beach in front of us.

A guy whose name tag read SGT. HARDY pointed down the sandy ridge to the ironwood trees that edged the beach. "You'll bivouac in those trees where you can't be seen from the sky."

In single file, we headed to the trees.

The ocean stretched away to dark reefs a quarter mile out, where small white waves crumpled on the sparkling blue water.

Ho! I thought. Sure beats Schofield.

"Set up your tents here," Sergeant Hardy said as more trucks arrived carrying mainland troops, who set up on the sandy ridge just above us.

"Why they don't come down here?" Chik asked.

Sergeant Hardy left without answering.

✛ ✛ ✛

Just after sunrise the next morning two trucks drove down into the ironwoods to our bivouac. Three men got out of the first truck and started tumbling roll after roll of barbed wire off the back end onto the sand.

The second truck carried picks, shovels, stacks of empty burlap sacks, boxes of ammunition, hand grenades, tripods, and three heavy water-cooled machine guns.

They unloaded all of it without a word to any of us. When they were done, they drove back up the sand dune.

An hour later, Sweet showed up. "You, you, and you," he said, pointing to me, Chik, and Slim. "Take two shovels and a third of these sacks and go up there above the high-tide line and dig out a pit big enough for two men and a machine gun. Do I have to tell you how to find the high-water mark?"

"No, sir," I said.

Sweet took the rest of the squad farther down the beach. The high-water line was easy to see, because of the beach debris the waves had pushed up.

A group of mainland soldiers sat around another machine-gun pit on the dune just above, watching us. Smart, I thought. If the enemy gets past us, those guys will get them. A second line of defense.

About six hundred yards down the beach, Sweet showed Cobra's group where to place their pit. And above them more mainland guys had set up a machine-gun hole. This part of the island would be well protected.

Slim and I shoveled sand into burlap sacks that Chik held open. As they filled up, he tied them off and stacked them around the edge of the pit.

"All we need now is the machine gun," I said.

"Maybe not going be us," Chik said. "Maybe we digging this for some mainland guys. Wouldn't surprise me."

I grunted. "That might make me mad."

✣ ✣ ✣

Sweet came over to scowl down on our pit. He moved a couple of sandbags, stamped others down with his boot. "Now go get a machine gun and a tripod. And bring over a box of ammo and nine hand grenades, three for each of you."

"See, Chik?" Slim said as we headed to the trees.

Sweet helped us lug the machine gun onto its tripod. He pried open the ammo box and showed us how to load the bandolier.

"Until further notice, this position belongs to you three," Sweet said. "Nothing comes up out of that ocean that isn't friendly, understand? I want two men in the pit at all times. Two hours on, four hours off, around the clock. Is that clear?"

It wasn't, but I could figure it out later.

"If they're smart, they'll come at night," Sweet said, gazing out to sea.

I squinted toward the ocean. The sky was turning dusky. Pale gray-blue clouds sat still on the horizon.

"Nobody dozes on his watch."

"Yes, sir."

"Everyone's kind of jumpy. Little hair-triggered, if you know what I mean."

I turned and looked up at the guys behind us.

"You sure you boys know how to work the MG?"

"Yes, sir," Slim said.

"Thing'll throw you clean out of that hole, you don't do it right, scrawny boys like you."

Slim was over six feet, as tall as Sweet himself. But I guess you could say me and Chik were small guys.

I blinked when Sweet's eyes dug into mine.

He shook his head, then started down the beach toward Cobra's pit.

But he stopped and walked back.

"One more thing—you see those men up on the dune?"

We turned to look behind us. "Yes, sir," I said. "The second line of defense, right?"

Sweet grinned. "Exactly."

He gazed up at the mainland guys and sucked his teeth, like some old Kaka'ako guy watching a card game.

"If the Japs land on this beach and you hesitate to shoot them, or if you even turn around and think about leaving your post, those men back there have orders to shoot you. You understand that? If the Nips come ashore and you take one step out of this hole, you're dead men, because I don't trust you. Am I making myself clear?"

Chik's jaw dropped. Slim wouldn't even look up. Blood boiled into my brain. We were soldiers in the United States Army! *Americans!* To say what he said was insane.

My fist opened and closed.

Wait, wait, wait, I told myself. Calm down. Do something stupid, you get court-martialed.

I felt like a fool, backing down like somebody's shoeshine boy.

Sweet headed over to Cobra's pit. "Look back and die, boys," he said over his shoulder.

78

16
THE HOLE

Late that night I sat in the hole with Chik, staring out onto an oil-black sea, one pair of binoculars between us.

Not knowing if we were going to be invaded was way worse than knowing, because my imagination was running wild. I could see the enemy scurrying in from the sea, quiet as rats—until the bullets flew, and then I got filled full of holes from the front *and* the back. Gave me the creeps. What would be worse, I wondered—getting shot in my chest or my back?

Stop thinking like that!

There was no moon. But deeper into the night the stars got so bright the ocean looked like a soft silver blanket. If the Japanese landed tonight, we would see them. And when they came dripping up out of the water with their bayonets gleaming in the starlight, we would be ready.

Chik nodded off.

I nudged him. "Come on, Chik. Stay awake."

"Yeah—yeah, I'm awake," he said, jolting up. Then he nodded off again.

"You can't *do* that. We're on watch."

"Okay, sure," he said, yawning and rubbing his face.

If the Japanese came, a lot of men would die, and I sure didn't want to be one of them. But not wanting to die wasn't cowardice. Cowardice was when you let your friends, or your island, or your country down, and no way would any of us do that.

There were no dark shapes out on the ocean. No sounds but the constant whoosh of waves slapping the sand.

But that didn't mean they weren't out there.

✣ ✣ ✣

I was on watch when the sun rose out on the horizon. Slim headed to his tent and Chik slid into the hole next to me, his helmet tumbling in ahead of him. Behind him I saw Sweet and another guy heading down the sandy knoll.

Chik's hair stuck up every which way. He rubbed his face, his breath sour.

"Put your helmet on, Sweet's coming—and check out who's with him."

Sweet and Captain Parrish walked up and stood over us. "Well, I'll be," Captain Parrish said. "Eddy Okubo, right? McKinley? Graduated early?"

"Yes, sir, that's me," I said.

"A promising shortstop, too, as I recall."

80

"Naah, my kid brother's the baseball player."

"So how'd it go last night?"

"No problems, sir."

"Kind of quiet?"

"Yeah."

"That's 'Yes, sir,' Private," Sweet snapped.

Captain Parrish raised his hand. "It's okay, Lieutenant."

Sweet's eyes carved me up.

Captain Parrish glanced back toward the men in the machine-gun pit above us. "Lieutenant, have those men up there move their hole up the beach about fifty yards. Way it is now puts these men right in their line of fire."

For long seconds Sweet didn't respond.

"Lieutenant?"

"Consider it done, sir."

"Good. We don't want to be shooting our own men."

"No, sir," Sweet said, his expression daring me to peep a word about what he'd told us last night.

Captain Parrish turned toward the ocean. "I think one man on watch along this stretch ought to do it during the day, Lieutenant. We need all the help we can rustle up to string wire."

"Yes, sir," Sweet said.

"Hey, Eddy," Captain Parrish said.

I looked up.

"When did you turn eighteen?"

I blinked. "Uh . . . last summer, sir."

He studied me with raised eyebrows, then half-grinned. "Glad to have you in the army, Private."

"Thank you, sir."

✥ ✥ ✥

For the next eight hours we strung double-apron barbed wire up and down the beach for miles in each direction. My muscles ached and salt stung the zillion scratches all over my arms, and all the time we worked, the mainland troops sat like mynah birds on the sandy hill, watching us.

That night I fell into my tent so beat I didn't even bother to slap mosquitoes.

✥ ✥ ✥

In the murky light of dawn the next morning I was in the hole with Slim when I saw something splashing around out in the water.

I grabbed the binoculars.

17
SAKAMAKI

"Something's out there," I said, handing the field glasses to Slim.

Slim panned the ocean until he found it. "Not something, somebody. Swimming, or . . . *wait!* . . . Ho! There's a small submarine out there, too—looks like it's stuck on the reef."

I grabbed the field glasses. It was a sub, all right, about a half mile out. But it was . . . strange, small, like a midget sub.

The sight of it made me so alert I could have heard a fish jump. I checked the swimmer, struggling, going down, coming up, going down. Straight off from Cobra's position.

"I'm going over to Cobra's hole." I tossed the binoculars back to Slim and I ran down the beach.

Cobra stood in the pit, motioning to four guys with

weapons racing down from the trees. "Somebody drowning out there!"

One guy stripped to his boxers, plunged in, and swam out.

The sun's glow lit the sky from below the horizon, the sky cloudless and steel blue. The sub was a black shadow out on the reef.

I crouched by Cobra.

"Japanese sub," he said. "And somebody in the water."

"Who's that swimming out?"

"Sergeant Akui."

He made it to the drowning guy about ten seconds after he went down for the last time. Sergeant Akui dove under and brought him back up.

I looked behind me, not wanting to get chewed out for leaving my hole. "Where's Sweet?"

Cobra shrugged.

The swimmer and Sergeant Akui slowly made it to shore and staggered out of the ocean, the Japanese guy stumbling, falling, coughing.

Ho, I thought. Now we going see the face of the enemy. Spooky.

He was naked, except for a white loincloth. His lips were blue and he was shivering, cold or scared or both.

"Samui, samui," he said, his teeth rattling. He struggled to bow and nod, stumbling up the sand.

"What did he say?" Sergeant Akui asked, his eyes searching ours. "Anybody."

"He said he's cold," Cobra said.

Sergeant Akui said to the seaman, " 'S okay, 's okay, we

not going hurt you. You," he called to Cobra. "Tell him not to worry. We won't shoot him."

Cobra spoke in his terrible Japanese.

The seaman bowed and bowed, and said something that made Cobra's jaw drop.

"Sergeant," Cobra said. "He says he *wants* you to shoot him."

"What?"

"He's deeply ashamed, because he was captured."

Sergeant Akui scowled. "Ask him his name."

Cobra did.

"Sakamaki," Cobra said.

"Ask him if there was anyone else in that sub with him."

"Yes. One more guy still out there. But he drowned. The sub—They got lost. They were supposed to be heading to Pearl Harbor."

Sergeant Akui called to three soldiers. "You men get a raft and go find the body. You," he said to Cobra. "Come with me. I need you to translate."

They walked up to the trees.

The guys in the raft brought the drowned guy in. His body was cut up from being snagged on the reef. They wrapped him in some blankets and took him away.

Sergeant Akui ordered me, Chik, and six more guys to go out to see if we could break the sub loose from the reef.

We dragged two rafts into the ocean and paddled out. The water was warm, the sun now climbing up over the edge of the world.

It was hard to imagine how two guys could fit in such a small sub. They'd have to be lying down. I couldn't do that,

I thought. To be trapped underwater inside a steel tube with no windows would drive me crazy. Enemy or not, I respected those guys. They were braver than I was.

"Hey," one guy said, tossing me a coil of rope. "Knot that around the tower."

I slipped into the ocean and swam to the sub, careful not to get cut up on the reef. I worked one end of the rope into a loop and flung it over the tower. The dull, dark steel was rough as sandpaper, a cold weapon of war.

We waited for the tide, and when the sub floated free we dragged it to shore.

All this time I couldn't get Sakamaki out of my head. He *wanted* us to shoot him. Pop was right about those guys. It shocked me to actually see that fighting spirit. But I understood it: Sakamaki lived by the *Bushido* code of the ancient warriors. The shame of surrender or capture was a disgrace.

I understood, because Sakamaki thought exactly like Pop.

18
ONE LAST LOOK

After more than a month in Waimanalo, me, Chik, and Cobra managed to wangle a twenty-four-hour pass home, the first we'd gotten since the bombs fell.

When I walked in the door, Opah yapped and jumped like a flea at my knees. Ma nearly fainted. I hadn't called to say I was coming.

"Hey, Ma," I said, rushing up to hug her. "I'm on pass till tomorrow night. How's things at home? Good, I hope."

She fanned her face with her hand, smiling shyly.

We sat on the old couch.

Opah leaped onto my lap, and I scratched his belly, his back leg flying.

Ma said, "How are you eating—"

"Never mind about me, Ma. I'm fine. Where's Pop and Herbie? At the shop?"

"Herbie's at school. Coming home soon. Your father is working, like always. Him and Bunichi."

She pushed herself up. "Come, I make you something to eat."

I knew that would make her feel good, so I followed her into the kitchen and let her fuss over me until Herbie came home.

"Heyyy," he said, smiling big.

I stood and slapped the side of his arm. "So catch me up on what's been going on, ah?"

We went outside and sat on the steps. Opah plopped down to sleep behind us.

"So, the truth," I said. "Everything all right here?"

Herbie nodded. "We don't see Pop too much, but other than that, everything is just like before."

"That's a relief."

"How about you?"

"Out at Waimanalo watching the beach."

"Sounds easy."

The Higashis' cat came up and rubbed against my leg. Opah lifted his head and the cat gave him a look. Opah put his head back down.

Man, it was good to be home. I stayed out on the porch with Herbie until it got dark.

When Pop came home, he started to grin when he saw me, but hid it, and nodded.

While we ate, I told him what I was doing, him grunting and nodding.

After dinner he went outside to sit on the steps like he did on most nights—watching people go by, sipping tea, sometimes carving a piece of wood. That night, I sat next to him.

"How's everything going, Pop?"

He thought so long I figured he wasn't going to answer. But then he said, "You good solja'?"

"Yeah, Pop, I'm a good soldier."

He nodded.

We sat.

"I sit in a sand pit and watch the ocean," I added.

Pop stared into the quiet Kaka'ako night.

So peaceful, so sweet, the cool air smelling like jasmine. I could have sat on those steps forever.

"In the paper I saw the guy, Sakamaki," Pop said out of the blue. "You saw him where you was?"

"I was there. He was a proud guy. He wanted us to shoot him."

Pop nodded.

Mr. and Mrs. Higashi walked by. They waved, and Pop raised his chin.

Then more silence.

"Boy," Pop said.

I waited.

"Me?" he said after a long pause. "I'm old country, yeah?"

"Yeah."

"But not you, I know."

I nodded.

"Ne'mind how I feel about Japan or what I want for you," he said. "What you doing now . . . it's right."

I couldn't have squeaked out a word if my life had depended on it.

✧ ✧ ✧

"Hey, Eddy, listen to this," Cobra said one morning, back in Waimanalo. He was reading a day-old newspaper in the speckled shade of the ironwood trees.

I was lying on my back with my eyes closed.

"They calling the states of Washington, Oregon, California, and the south part of Arizona military sites, now."

"How come?"

He read, *"The prospect that enemy aliens and persons of Japanese ancestry will be removed therefrom is good common sense."* He put the paper down. "That means—"

"They kicking every Japanese out of all those *states*?"

"That's what it says."

He read more: *"Any large-scale evacuation of these areas cannot but impose hardship on countless innocent and law-abiding persons, but that is the way of war—and this country did not start it."*

We looked at each other, then turned away. Cobra crumpled up the paper and threw it as far as he could.

✧ ✧ ✧

For almost five months we guarded an empty sea. Then, in May, we were called back to Schofield.

"You grunts are shipping out," Sweet said. "Who knows where? But you'd be smart to prepare yourselves, physically and mentally, because I'd say you boys are looking at combat, and that means some of you won't be heading back this way. So you might want to take one last look around."

Combat.

That nightmare word and the smile in Sweet's eyes were like the snap and fizz of a fast-burning fuse.

19
THE BLUE
STONE

On June 5, 1942, the army loaded us onto the sugarcane train and sent us down to Iwilei Depot, near Honolulu Harbor—1,432 island troops.

Finally, they were letting us be real soldiers. I was proud to stand up for something I believed in, no matter what guys like Sweet thought.

But still, I was scared.

Who would I be when I was looking down the barrel of some German rifle? Or worse, a Japanese one. Who would I be then? A soldier? Or a coward?

From the depot, we marched with all our gear to the pier, where we were to board the USAT *Maui,* a transport ship.

The minute I'd heard we were shipping out to the mainland, I called Mrs. Higashi and asked her to tell my family. When I saw Ma at the harbor with Herbie I felt overwhelmingly sad. I was about to leave the island—for the first time in my life.

Herbie stood solemnly with his hands jammed into his pockets. His T-shirt and bare feet reminded me of everything I was leaving behind. From here on my life would be made up of things and places I'd never known before.

Ma, wearing a gray dress and black sweater, looked shrunken into herself.

I hugged her. "Where's Pop?"

"Working." She looked off to nowhere, her eyes glistening with tears.

Herbie moved closer, surrounding her with his arm, something I'd never seen him do before. It both relieved and saddened me to know that he had grown a couple of years in the past few months.

I let my barracks bag drop off my shoulder.

Ma looked everywhere but at me, pressing a white handkerchief to her mouth.

"Ma," I said softly. "I going be okay. Please . . . don't worry."

She closed her eyes and tears squeezed out.

"Herbie," I said. "Write to me, okay? Every couple of weeks, if you can. Let me know what's going on. I'll write, too."

Herbie dropped his arm off Ma's shoulder and glanced away.

"What?" I said.

"You better come back . . . I mean . . . when it's over."

I reached out and ruffled his hair. "You got it, little man."

Herbie smiled, though he tried not to. He dug into his pocket. "Here."

"What's this?"

"A good-luck charm."

I took the deep blue stone, polished smooth, like turquoise, but darker. "Where'd you get this?"

"You know that team we play, the Rats?"

"Yeah."

"Well, the pitcher, you know, the haole—Billy? I won that stone off him in a bet."

"You made a bet with a haole?"

"Why not?"

I shrugged. "What is this? Turquoise?"

"Lapis. That's what Billy said. I like the color. You don't see stones like that around here."

"Sure don't."

I rubbed it between my finger and thumb, then dropped it into my pocket. "I'll carry it everywhere. Thanks, Herbie."

We glanced into each other's eyes, then quickly looked away. It wasn't something we usually did. We weren't like that. But we were getting that way.

I shook his hand, then pulled him close and hugged him. So what if the guys saw? Who cared?

"Write," I said.

"Yeah."

I turned to Ma, who still wouldn't look at me. "I'll be back for sure," I said, then hugged her.

She shook her head, the handkerchief still pressed to her mouth. She was trembling.

It tore me up, but I had to go.

I headed onto the gangway with my platoon and Sweet, who was still with us, barking orders, scowling.

Halfway up I glanced back one last time. I nearly ran back down when I saw Ma gazing up at the ship, her hands reaching toward me, almost lost in the waving crowd.

✛ ✛ ✛

A few hours later we were steaming out of Honolulu with news that a huge battle between the U.S. and Japan was raging to the west, at Midway Island. If the Japanese won, they'd take Hawaii next.

That thought almost made me jump overboard and swim home. Ma, Herbie, and Pop were the ones who had to be brave, not me. The monster was looking down *their* throats.

For the first time in years, tears fell from my eyes.

20
TRIP TO
NOWHERE

We headed to San Francisco, berthed three decks down, where the air was stale and stank like fuel. We slept in triple-stacked canvas bunks with less than two feet between them. The lightbulbs were dim and the portholes were blacked out. Before the first day was over, half of us were so seasick we couldn't even stand up.

So, so miserable.

Day after day.

But when Admiral Nimitz announced in a radio address broadcast over the loudspeakers that the U.S. had defeated the Japanese at Midway, the whole ship broke out in the longest cheer I'd ever heard in my life. For now, our families were safe.

It had been a long time since I'd felt that good.

✠ ✠ ✠

On June 10, we slipped under the Golden Gate Bridge, so big and so high I couldn't believe anybody could have built it.

But even better was all that land—solid ground—sunshine, clean air, green hills on one side, biggest city I ever saw on the other.

We docked in Oakland, and the second we got off the ship, me, Chik, Cobra, and about three hundred other soldiers dropped to our knees and kissed the pavement.

Before we could get back up, armed troops swooped down on us.

"Move along!" they shouted, herding us away from the civilian families who had sailed with us. The troops, Sweet among them, marched us onto three different trains.

"Keep the window shades down," Sweet said as I stowed my gear and found a place to sit. "We don't need people seeing you and panicking over a train full of Japs."

That did it.

"Sir," I said. "You wrong to call us Japs. Japs are the ones who bombed Pearl Harbor—the enemy, not us. We're Americans."

Boom!

Sweet had me in the aisle.

"Fifty push-ups, Private, then fifty more. I want you down there licking spit until your arms fall off. You hear me? Private? You hear what I said?"

"Yes, sir!"

"I don't take insubordination of any kind. You don't talk back to a superior. You do that again, you're in the brig, understand?"

"Yes, sir!" I spat.

His boots were planted an inch from my face. I glanced up. His face was red and veins bulged in his neck. I thought he was going to kick me.

He spun around and slammed down the aisle to the next car.

When he was gone I got up, rubbing my burning arms. "Fool," I mumbled.

"We going to prison," Cobra said. "They tricked us into thinking we were going to fight!"

"But why, Cobra?" Chik said.

"You watch."

I fell into a seat.

Two armed guards came in and pushed down the aisle, studying us. I lowered my gaze when one of them locked on me.

The train jerked ahead, and I soon fell asleep.

I woke with a jump when, sometime later, the train squealed and jolted to a stop.

I lifted the shade and peeked out. A station.

Not twenty feet from my window, a crew of workers were digging with picks and shovels.

"Hey, come look," I said.

Chik, Cobra, and PeeWee squeezed in around me.

It was a shock. Never in our lives had we seen white guys doing pick-and-shovel work.

Cobra clicked his tongue. "Prisoners, ah? Must be a chain gang."

"But no guards," Chik said.

He was right. They were free men.

The train moved on.

Sweet let us raise the shades when we weren't in some town or city, and ho, what a sight. I'd never been anywhere that I couldn't see the ocean. It was the strangest feeling to be *inside* the land. Trapped in it. We were islanders, used to small places. Only because we knew the ocean did we understand endlessness like this—mountains far away in the hazy distance, dry desert, red hills, miles and miles of pastures, cows, horses, farmland so perfect it looked fake. Amazing.

On and on, the train clicking along the tracks, with nothing from Sweet about where we were going. *Click, click, click*—the sound lulling me to sleep—until I realized something and popped awake. My birthday had come and gone on that ship!

I was seventeen.

✤ ✤ ✤

Days later, when we just about couldn't take it anymore, we crossed into a green land of forests, lakes, cows, and no mountains.

"You're in Wisconsin, grunts," Sweet said, finally giving us something. "Anyone ever heard of it?"

"Only all of us, you fool," Cobra mumbled.

When the train stopped, I peeked out the window.

Yah!

My scalp prickled. Felt like my hair rose straight up. Cobra was right—prison was right outside the window!

Faces peered back at us through a chain-link fence—Japanese faces. And one face I could hardly believe.

A guy standing off by himself.

Sakamaki.

Chik and Cobra shoved in around me. We gaped at him. And all those people. So sad, so beaten. A fire burned in my throat.

"It's really true," Cobra whispered.

"Can't be," Chik said. "No."

But there was the proof—Sakamaki. The guy we'd captured at Waimanalo.

A feeling of complete emptiness washed over me. The feeling you get when you give up.

But the train jolted and moved ahead.

Sakamaki's fingers clutched the chain-link fence as we pulled away. He glared at us, his face strangely pockmarked. His eyes were fierce. Probably he still wanted to be shot.

But the rest of those faces seemed hopeless and confused. Men and women, young, old. Who were they? What crime had they committed?

We looked at them and they looked back, and something passed between us—something like deep, deep sorrow.

But not Sakamaki. He lived in another world.

The train stopped for the last time less than a mile down the line.

From there we were bussed into Camp McCoy, a sprawling army reservation of fields, forests, creeks, and low hills. Tall trees framed the camp itself, a tidy place.

But back in the far corner of the camp was the prison. An internment center, they called it. Except for Sakamaki, it wasn't a place for enemies but for people the government had kicked out of all those West Coast states.

Just people. Americans.

21
CAMP MCCOY

The air at Camp McCoy was fresh and sweet, and the summer sun blazed hot, just like at home.

Cobra looked the place over with his usual squint. PeeWee and Golden Boy broke out their cards, and Chik wondered if there were any good-looking girls in town.

"Now, this is more like it," I said, because for the first time since any of us had been in the army, we slept in bunks with springs and mattresses and stored our gear in footlockers, and best of all, enjoyed clean latrines—*inside* the barracks.

One night after chow, Chik fell back on his bunk with his hands behind his head. "This is the life, ah?"

"Pfff," Cobra scoffed. "Fools are so easily pleased, ah, Eddy?"

I laughed and headed outside to sit on the steps to write a letter to Herbie.

I thought for a long time before I wrote, remembering what home looked like. Kaka'ako, the harbor, the boatyard. Sharky and Opah. Ma and Herbie. Bunichi.

And Pop. What was he doing now? Rebuilding the *Red Hibiscus*? Would they let him do that?

Maybe.

But mostly I wondered if he ever thought about me.

Dear Herbie,

Well, we made it to the mainland without getting hit by a torpedo. We had to zigzag all the way to San Francisco. The week on that ship was the worst week I ever had in my life. Everyone got seasick and had to throw up all the time, sometimes on each other. But we made it. Now we're at an army camp where we're going through basic training all over again. But I like it here. I wish I could tell you where we are.

So tell me, how's Pop? Did he ever find out why the sampan burned? I don't know about you, but I think about that all the time. Boats don't just burn up like that. What's he doing now? Rebuilding it?

Except for the food, the army is okay. But I don't think I'm going to stay in it when my time is up. I don't think they want us anyway. They won't miss me.

Write me and tell me what's going on at home. Tell me everything, okay? And tell Ma I'm doing fine and not to worry.

Don't forget.

Write back.

Oh, and thanks for that stone. I got it in my pocket right now.

Eddy

✣ ✣ ✣

Three weeks later, we were designated the Hundredth Infantry Battalion, and for the first time our platoon leaders were Japanese, not white guys. We still had Sweet, and Mr. Parrish joined us, too. He was a major now.

The only bad part about Camp McCoy was the endless boot camp. Everyone else in the U.S. Army was fighting in Europe and the Pacific. But not us, not the guys who looked like Hirohito. We just kept on training.

"This is nuts," I said one day, sitting around with Chik and Cobra. "They never going let us fight in this war, so why not just send us home?"

"You dreaming," Cobra said. "Here they got us under control, ah? If we was home, they would worry about us again. Think about it."

Me and Chik nodded.

"All one game, this," Cobra said.

"Yeah, but if we was in Europe, would be ugly," Chik said. "War ain't pretty."

"But at least we could do our part, ah?" I said. "Prove we loyal."

"That what you are?" Cobra said.

I glared at him. "Of course. You not?"

Cobra turned away. "Yeah, I am, but this is . . ."

I nodded, thinking if they ever let us fight in this war, I will stand up and go to the end.

They're not going to crush me, no.

Ganbare! Persevere!

That was what Pop would do.

One dark, cold night I lay on my bunk, sleepless. It was after midnight.

I heard a creak and popped up on my elbow.

Two men stood in the doorway, their silhouettes outlined by a glowing bulb outside the open door.

They waited a few seconds, then came inside.

They went from bunk to bunk, waking one guy here, one there. But not everyone. They woke Chik, Shig, Cobra.

I recognized one of the intruders as Ricky Kondo, a college Rotsie from Maui. Because of his education, they'd made him a lieutenant.

The shape of the other guy was unmistakable.

Sweet.

They woke Slim, Ray, James, Tokuji.

Each guy got up and went quietly to his footlocker.

But some guys they left alone.

What *was* this?

They woke Hot Dog, Golden Boy, Koji.

Sweet headed toward me. Faint light from the open door reflected off the brass on his uniform.

I sat up. The metal springs under my mattress squeaked.

"Get all your gear together," he said. "Everything. Assemble outside in field dress in five minutes. And be quiet about it."

I got up. Dressed quickly.

Out of habit I made my bed, then jammed everything from my footlocker into my barracks bag.

Outside, the air stung my face, cold and sharp. Ghost-like smoke swirled when I breathed. The other barracks and the roads between them and the trees that lined the compound were lit by a few dim bulbs. Two personnel trucks idled nearby. The only other sounds were the padded footfalls of guys falling in.

No one spoke.

Relief surged through me when I saw that I was still with Chik and Cobra.

Ricky Kondo came out of the barracks and stood on the top step. He shook his head, a small private signal that meant he didn't know much more about what all this was than we did. Just following orders.

Sweet ducked out behind him. He studied us, eyes hard, lips tight.

What was going on?

He came down off the steps to review us. When he got to me, he stopped.

Ever since that time I'd corrected him on the train, he'd been watching me, ready to take me down.

Look at a spot on the bridge of his big fat nose, I told myself. Anywhere but his eyes. Hold your breath if you have to. Think of the beach. Think of Sharky growling at Cobra. Think of anything, but don't look in his eyes and don't blink.

Sweet grinned and moved on.

When he finally spoke, it was in his quiet voice, the one that made you worry.

"Listen up, because I'm only saying this once. When I dismiss you, take your gear and go get on those two troop trucks yonder. Don't nobody speak to nobody or try to go back into the barracks to say goodbye to your buddies. Just get on the trucks. Quick and quiet."

A distant train blew its whistle, echoing through the night.

"Dismissed."

I grabbed my barracks bag and tossed it onto one of the trucks, then climbed in. A bench ran along each side, and a heavy canvas tarp covered the top.

I moved forward and sat with my gear between my feet. More guys piled in.

Why only twenty-five guys? And why *us* twenty-five?

Sweet peeked into the truck. "I'm tying down this tarp. Keep it that way."

Now I couldn't see anything. Even when my eyes adjusted, I could barely make out the shape of the guy across from me.

Up front, both cab doors thumped shut. We lurched forward, the sickly smell of diesel exhaust seeping in under the tarp. I held my breath as long as I could.

The hum of the engine made me doze off, the first sleep I'd had that night. I dreamed about the easy blue sea, and Sharky, licking engine oil off parts in Pop's boatyard.

I was jarred awake sometime later when the truck stopped and sat idling, diesel fumes drifting back in.

Sweet threw open the flap.

We were backed up to a doorway. Inside, there was light.

"What you're looking at," Sweet said, "is the inside of a DC-3. That's an airplane. Take your gear and step over into it."

Not one of us had ever in our lives been this close to an airplane.

"Let's go," Sweet said.

The plane sat with its back end slanting down and its front rising to the cockpit. The window shades were down and the cockpit door was open to a city of glowing red dials. The pilot and copilot were turned in their seats, watching us come on board.

I threw my barracks bag up into a bin and sat.

Ricky looked irritated, his face pinched. I didn't blame him. He was a lieutenant, and still nobody was telling him anything.

I lifted my shade a few inches. Not too far away was a hangar lit by one light, its huge door open to black emptiness inside.

I jumped when a guard on the ground outside tapped on my window with his rifle. Ho, where'd *he* come from? He scowled and motioned for me to pull the shade back down.

The other truck arrived and loaded the rest of us onto the DC-3.

Sweet got on last, pulling the door shut behind him.

The pilots fired up the props, making a terrible racket. I reached into my pocket for my good-luck stone: You better be working today.

The DC-3 started to move. All around me guys had mempachi eyes, big and bugged-out like that fish. We picked up speed, going faster and faster down the runway. Had to be a hundred miles an hour, or a thousand, I don't know.

The plane groaned into the sky. I felt like I weighed two hundred pounds. Up and up, bouncing, rattling, shaking. We tilted, straightened, went up some more, and with my eyes pinched shut and my fingers digging into the seat, I begged that I would please, please, please step on solid ground just one more time in my life.

23
SUGAR BABE

With shades down, the DC-3 droned on.

Chik and Cobra slept.

But I was wide awake, rubbing that blue stone and wondering if I had the guts to peek out the window. What was out there, so high up? Clouds? Angels? Ghosts?

I checked Sweet, then inched up the window shade.

Ho!

Far below, the long silver-colored serpent of a river snaked across the land. The sun was just rising in the east, spreading long shadows over green fields, pastures, lakes, and forests. The view was so big I could hardly take it all in. Never had I seen anything like it before.

I pulled the shade back down and tried to sleep.

I woke with a jump when I felt the plane going down. I grabbed that blue stone quick.

Down, down.

I stopped breathing.

When the wheels thumped back on earth, we shouted and clapped and joked about how easy flying was.

"Knock it off," Sweet shouted.

The urge to raise the shade and peek out was so strong I had to sit on my hands.

Sweet stood. "Grab your gear, grunts. We're getting off. Kondo, take the lead."

The pilot ducked out of the cockpit and hunched back to open the door. Thick, warm air rushed in, soft and thick and warm as the air back home.

Outside, two more army troop trucks waited for us. Otherwise, the airfield was deserted.

"Where are we?" Lieutenant Kondo asked Sweet.

"Mississippi."

I squinted into the distance, thinking I'd seen something move. What I saw jarred me. Armed MPs were positioned around the edges of the entire field, standing back in the morning shadows.

"Move along. Let's go."

We boarded the trucks and headed away from the air-field.

After we'd been driving awhile, PeeWee said, "You smell that?"

I sniffed the air.

"Salt water," Cobra said.

When the truck came to a stop, Sweet looked in on us. "One more ride, grunts . . . then you're home."

We jumped off the truck.

We were at a harbor, with sunny ocean beyond. A wharf, or a pier. "Yes," I whispered.

But again, MPs lurked in the shadows.

No civilians anywhere. No workers, no fishermen.

What is this?

Chik lifted his chin toward the harbor. "Man, that sight is like honey on my tongue," he said, shading his eyes from the sun.

Boats sat motionless in their slips. Outriggers and antennas stabbed into the air, looking just like the fishing boats back home. The sea beyond was light blue and calm, and the sweet stink of dead fish whispered in my nose.

Sweet headed out onto the pier to see the skipper of one of the boats. As they talked, the skipper kept glancing back at us.

A few minutes later, Sweet returned. "Lucky us. We got an easy sea today."

"We going on that boat?" Ricky Kondo asked.

"Grab your gear."

I tossed my barracks bag over my shoulder. We filed out onto the pier.

The boat was white with black trim—the same colors as the *Red Hibiscus*. But this one had rust stains leaking from its water ports. It needed new paint. Looked to me about forty-five feet. *Sugar Babe, Gulfport* was arced across the transom. A fishing boat, but not sampan style.

"Meet Leroy," Sweet said. "Your skipper."

Leroy nodded and helped us find spots for our gear. He was maybe an inch taller than me, and his skin was burned leathery brown by the sun. He had a craggy face, spiky black whiskers, and a powerful odor. But he seemed like an okay guy. He smiled a lot.

When everyone was jammed aboard, Leroy fired up the engines, unhitched the dock lines, and walked the boat out of the harbor. That was one of the best moments I'd had since I joined the U.S. Army.

I stood facing the breeze, sucking in thick, salty air. Chee, did it feel good to be on a fishing boat again.

Sweet settled in a spot near the wheel, by Leroy. He sat with a sigh, leaned his head back, closed his eyes.

"Hey, Eddy, look," Cobra said, glancing back at the MPs on the dock. "Don't matter where we go, ah? Same like always."

I shaded my eyes and saw people emerging from dark places in the buildings—fishermen and dockworkers coming out into the sunlight to watch our boat head out to sea.

"Lieutenant," PeeWee said, "where we going now?"

Sweet peeked open one eye, smiled, and went back to sleep.

24
SHIP ISLAND

Soon a long, low island appeared on our starboard side.

Leroy said, "This here water's what we call the Mississippi Sound. As you can see, it's kind of muddy. That's from the rivers. The water in the sound is brackish, fresh from the rivers, mixed in with salt from the other side of the island. On that side you got your Gulf of Mexico, and that's all salt."

"This island got a name?" Chik asked.

"Yep, Cat Island. French named it. They found raccoons there and thought they was giant cats." He chuckled.

Cat Island ran east to west and looked to be about three miles long—an island of tall trees and thick jungle undergrowth. The shore was a thin line of sand and marsh grass. Nothing else. No people and no houses, as far as I could see.

We watched it slip silently by.

Ahead, another island grew up out of the water. Flatter. Looked like a sandbar, with a lighthouse and a huge fortlike thing on it. Way down at the other end, tall trees stood hazy in the purple distance.

Leroy motioned toward a long pier fingering out into the water. The big fort was at the end of it.

"This island here's called Ship. That there is old Fort Massachusetts, built back in the Civil War. After the war, it was used as a quarantine station for yellow fever."

Leroy throttled down and headed toward the pier. The lighthouse was off to the left, about a quarter mile down the coast. Just beyond the fort were a couple of shacks.

That was it. You could walk from one side of the island to the other in five minutes. All of us were standing now as Leroy eased the boat alongside the pier.

Sweet grinned. "Welcome home, miserable grunts."

Cobra spat over the side, his face shiny with sweat. "Look like one big wave could roll right over this island."

"Shuddup," Chik said. "Now you put that thought in my head."

"Or maybe an earthquake could sink it."

"You'll be okay," Leroy said. "Only time to worry is if there's a hurricane."

"Thanks," Chik said, scowling. "I feel better now."

But today the ocean was as flat as a puddle.

Sweet jumped off and secured the dock lines. We tossed up our gear and climbed off. I took a deep breath. Wow—a paradise. All we needed were a few trees to sit under, maybe a couple of hammocks.

"Ho, look!" Chik said.

116

In the shallow water off the pier was a school of fish, right below us, with their torpedo-shaped backs lounging in the quiet water. Everyone crowded around to see—except Sweet, who was already heading up to the shacks.

"White sea trout," Leroy said.

"Man, I could catch fifty at one time," I said. "If I had my net."

Cobra scoffed. "What are you fools talking about? You think they brought us here to go fishing?"

Chik stared at him. "What's wrong now? This ain't so bad to me."

"What you think we doing here?" Cobra said.

Chik shrugged.

"That's right, you don't know, and Ricky don't know either, do you, Ricky?"

"Nope."

"Don't it seem strange that Sweet won't even tell another lieutenant what's going on?"

"Maybe it's top-secret," Chik said.

Cobra threw up his hands. "I give up."

"What I did?"

"Nothing. Let's go."

We lugged our gear to the shacks. We had enough food and fresh water for a week or so.

Sweet waited for us at the biggest shack, holding the screen door open. "This way, gents."

The place was dusty and crawling with small black spiders. There was a kitchen, a small room for supplies, and one big room with folding spring-frame cots and thin brownish mattresses stacked against one wall. Blankets, sheets, and pillows were heaped under a tarp in a corner. There was a small woodstove, with a pile of wood out back, and running well water that smelled like a swamp in the kitchen. I couldn't imagine drinking it. Outside was a latrine with a shower.

"Get set up and make yourselves at home," Sweet said. "I'm going over to Gulfport with the skipper. Someone will be back with your orders in a day or two. Until then, Lieutenant Kondo's in charge."

"But sir," I said. "What are we *doing* here?"

Sweet opened the screen door.

Ricky Kondo stared at the floor, the muscles in his jaw working, looking like he wanted to strangle Sweet.

Sweet winked. *"Sayonara."*

The door slapped shut behind him.

25
CAT ISLAND

Ricky Kondo put his hands on his hips. "Could be worse, I guess. Let's get this place cleaned up."

Hot Dog and Koji, a guy from Molokai, were assigned to do all the cooking. Golden Boy became our censor; he would make sure that the letters we wrote didn't give our location or assignment away.

"What?" Chik grumbled. "You mean he going read *every* letter we write?"

"Every last one," Ricky Kondo said.

Golden Boy wagged his eyebrows. "No worry, Chickaboom. Nobody but me will ever know."

"Ain't right," Chik spat. "I going read yours, then."

"No hold your breath, son."

I did my work as fast as I could, wanting to get outside

and look around. "Hey, Chik," I said. "How's about we go check inside that fort?"

"Naah, I going take a nap."

I asked Cobra, but he'd found an old bamboo pole and was heading out to do some fishing.

"I thought you said we wasn't doing no fishing here," Chik said.

"Changed my mind."

"Pfff," Chik said, shaking his head. "You something, you know?"

I thought, I just might like this place.

✢ ✢ ✢

Leroy came back four days later. By then we were as sunburned as a bunch of kids who didn't have enough sense to start looking for shade. This naked island baked—the only shade was inside the barrack.

Still, we had fish galore and plenty of fresh air. Even Cobra was his old self again. But we couldn't shake that unsettled feeling, wondering why we were here.

When we saw the *Sugar Babe* heading toward us, we all went down to the pier.

Leroy walked the boat in and tossed up a line. The *Sugar Babe* rose and fell gently, engine rumbling low.

"Morning," he said. "I'm here to bring y'all over to Cat Island today. Some men are waiting for you."

"What men?" Ricky Kondo asked.

"Couple guys I never met before. Just dropped 'em off. Oh . . . they said bring your boots."

We went back and shook the bugs out of our boots and returned to board the *Sugar Babe*. Only Hot Dog and Koji stayed behind, because all they had to do was cook.

Leroy sure hadn't lost his appetite for talking. He didn't smell any better, either. But I liked him.

"Don't y'all worry none," he said, easing the *Sugar Babe* away from the pier. "You're gonna like Cat Island. Used to go fishing there. Then the war broke out and the army told folks to stay away. They got kennels there, you know. Top-secret, I guess."

"Kennels?" Chik said. "Like for dogs?"

"Dogs on Cat Island," Leroy said, grinning. "Ain't that a hoot? They was all somebody's house pets, those dogs. Then when the war broke out their owners volunteered them for the army, just like you boys was volunteered, huh?"

"Yeah," Chik said, "but some dumb guys joined up on their own." He winked at me.

I shook my head.

"Hey, be nice, Chik," Ricky Kondo said.

"What? You joined up, too?"

"Yep."

"Shee, hard to believe."

Leroy chuckled at us.

Then his face went grim. "You boys are lucky, though. Over in Europe kids like you are dying by the truckload. Civilians, too. I just read that the Nazis have killed more than a quarter million people in occupied Europe."

We fell silent, the number staggering.

It's where we should have been, fighting over there, helping those people, I thought.

Mississippi broke up in heat waves on our starboard side. We gazed at its long coastline until Leroy changed the subject.

"See right where that big white warehouse is? That's Gulfport, where I come from. And down back thataway is Biloxi. I'd be glad to show you boys around if you ever get some shore leave."

"Yeah," I said. "That would be good."

A half hour later we were running parallel to Cat Island. On the east end was a branch of white beach that sat on the island like the head on a hammer. The long handle was all jungle.

Leroy squinted toward the marshes and tall trees on shore. There were no piers or buildings or people.

"I'da took y'all to the far side where there's a pier, but I can't let you off there. It's a whole lot easier, but they said I got to let you off on this side. Still, it's shallow, and I can get in close enough for y'alls to wade ashore."

The rippled-sand bottom slipped by no more than three feet below. The water was the color of rust.

Leroy swung the wheel around when he spotted two men in the trees along the shore.

The *Sugar Babe* inched closer. Leroy shut the engine down and dug up an old anchor. He grinned and nodded to the port side. "Don't mind those visitors, now."

A pack of twenty or thirty stingrays swooped toward the boat. "Cow rays is what those are. All's they are is curious. They won't bite, nope."

Shig cringed.

Chik said, "You want us to step into *that*?"

122

"Sure. They'll make a space for you."

Cobra grabbed his boots and tied them together by the laces. He tossed them over his shoulder and slid into the water.

The cow rays scattered.

Cobra, thigh-deep, looked up at us. "Jump in, cowards."

On shore, the two men waited.

One by one we dropped over the side with our boots and slogged toward the island, cow rays sailing around us.

The warm water felt good, sucking my pants up against my legs. Soft sand squirted between my toes.

One guy waved as we approached.

Major Parrish.

Up on the sand, fiddler crabs raced away under our feet, their pinchers open, ready to fight. Rotted stumps stuck up along the shore, a dense jungle just inland.

"Welcome to Cat Island, men."

26
THE SECRET MISSION

Major Parrish turned and motioned to the white-haired man behind him. The guy wore a uniform with no insignias, brass, or stripes. He was red in the cheeks and had wild blue eyes.

"This is Franz," Major Parrish said. "He's Swiss."

Franz nodded.

We mumbled hello, standing in a semicircle, half of us ankle-deep in the water.

Somebody's got to explain something soon, I thought. This is getting crazy.

"I apologize for all the secrecy," Major Parrish said, as if he'd read my mind. "But it had to be that way. What you'll be doing here is experimental, and secret."

He looked down at his boots.

Buying time, I thought.

He rubbed his chin and looked up. "A few months ago a German sub popped up off Long Island, New York. A small platoon of highly trained spies and saboteurs with explosives and detonators came ashore in an inflatable boat. It was foggy, and they were well hidden.

"Several days later it happened again off the coast of Florida. Four more enemy agents came ashore. Fortunately, the FBI captured all of these men before they could do the damage they had in mind.

"We have thousands of miles of coastline, and to protect all of it is just about impossible. But we must. And to do this we need the most alert sentries we can find. We also need them where we're fighting in the jungles of the Pacific."

Major Parrish paused. "That's why you're here, men."

Sentries? *That's* why we're here?

Why not? I thought. We know about the coast, and the ocean. But why here? We could have done this at Camp McCoy. And why only us? They need way more than twenty-five guys; twenty-six if you count Lieutenant Kondo.

Cobra stared at the sand, his hands on his hips. I could almost hear his bad thoughts.

Major Parrish went on. "This might be called Cat Island, but there are no cats here. There are, however, dogs—U.S. Army war dogs—and these dogs are going to fill that need."

Now I was really confused.

"The dogs are here under the direction of the Quartermaster Corps. Your particular mission will be to help prepare them for use in warfare. They will be trained as messenger dogs, scout dogs, sentry dogs, suicide dogs, and attack dogs. Franz is in charge of the program," he said, turning toward the Swiss guy.

This is great, I thought. I liked dogs.

"Major," Ricky Kondo said. "I hope you understand that none of us ever trained dogs before."

Major Parrish shook his head. "No, no, Lieutenant, the trainers are from the Quartermaster Corps. They're called handlers, and they're already at work here. You're going to . . . help them."

Shig said, "Sir, how come you didn't set us up on this island, then? Would be easier."

Major Parrish nodded. "Franz thought it best to keep you separated from the dogs. You see, each handler has been developing a relationship with his dogs, taking them through a sort of dog boot camp. Now the training gets more serious. Now they need you, and your part is very important, so important that they can't proceed without you. But it's imperative that you not be around the dogs when you aren't working with them. They only answer to their handlers, and it would confuse them to see too much of you. Is that right, Franz?"

Franz nodded. "Precisely."

Major Parrish hesitated. "You see, men . . . you are here to represent the enemy these dogs will encounter in the Pacific. We're going to train them to find you by your Japanese scent. You're not the trainers . . . you're . . . you're the bait. We're going to teach them to smell you, track you down, and attack you."

126

27
BAIT

Something blew inside me.

Bait? We were nothing but *bait*?

In the dead silence I staggered.

"They're not going to hurt you, of course," Major Parrish went on. "We're going to simulate it, but rest assured, no one's going to get hurt."

It was the *Red Hibiscus* all over again. Take it out on the Japs.

A muscle in Cobra's cheek twitched, his unblinking eyes fixed on Major Parrish.

Pop. What should I do?

Then I thought, No, I could *never* tell him. Dog bait.

What was worse was, the news was coming from Major Parrish, who I had trusted.

"Listen," Major Parrish said. "It's not as bad as it sounds.

At first, all you're going to do is hide in the jungle and let dogs find you. Those of you working with the attack dogs and sentry dogs may have to wear some protective gear after a while, but that's about it."

Cobra glanced at me, jaw tight, muscles working.

I shook my head slightly.

"The important thing," Major Parrish went on, "is that if these dogs can be trained to smell the enemy, and to attack them on command, they might save our soldiers' lives."

Our soldiers? Who were we? Nothing but raw meat?

Franz stood with his chin on his chest and his arms crossed.

Major Parrish went on. "This program has been authorized by President Roosevelt, and I expect you as U.S. Army soldiers to do your job and do it well. I know you will, and that's why I handpicked each one of you for this assignment."

Mr. Parrish! I shouted in my head. I thought you respected us!

"Follow me," he said. "I'll show you the dogs."

✣ ✣ ✣

Waist-high grass reached in over a sandy trail that took us toward the interior.

Bait.

The word banged around inside me trying to find a place to settle. Fire brewed in my veins. I knew Cobra felt it, too, heat fanned by wild winds.

Between the pines and scrub bushes, palmetto trees

sprouted like bursting fireworks. Wiry gray oaks wore branches bearded with moss.

We came to a pond. Long marsh grasses crowded the edges. The water was so still and clear, you could see the shadows of surface bugs on the bottom.

Major Parrish stopped. "Be careful in bayous and water-ways like this. There's alligators on this island. They like to hide in the long grass."

We edged the pond carefully.

The trail ended at the Quartermaster camp, where hundreds of tidy dog kennels lined up on cleared ground, wooden boxes with chicken-wire doors.

Men tending the dogs stopped and looked up as we approached. To the left, tents sprawled into the trees.

For the first time, the Swiss guy spoke to us.

"On the days we need you, that same boat will pick you up and drop you off where it did today. You will hike in and wait here. Your handlers will meet you and tell you what to do. But this is as close as you will ever get to the kennels. Everything beyond this point is off-limits. To these dogs you will never be a friend. You are the enemy."

He let those words hang in the air.

"We want them to hate you, you see. That's the goal."

28
KOOCH

It took me a day or two to settle with the idea of being dog bait. Cobra wouldn't talk to anyone. Chik wrote letters that he stashed under his pillow, not ready to let Golden Boy censor them.

"How can we be dog bait, PeeWee?" I said, the two of us sitting on a small hill of sand, watching Shig and Golden Boy pound each other in a sandball fight. "I mean, we supposed to be soldiers. Right?"

"All I know is it's orders, so we gotta do it."

I squinted at Shig and Golden Boy, so easily having fun, not even thinking about it.

"If we don't do it," PeeWee added, "then we going see the inside of some lousy brig, ah? Have a court-martial. Take away our stripes."

I laughed. "Stripes?"

"Well, we got one."

"They can have it."

But the brig would be even worse shame than dog bait. Pop would never be able to lift his head again. Me, either.

"Listen," PeeWee said. "Don't think about it. Just do it. That's what I going do. Ain't no big deal. So we the bait. Why fight it? Only bring trouble."

"Yeah."

Right then I decided, I'm a U.S. Army soldier. I'll do my duty just as I said I would. But who said I had to like it?

"How come they think we smell different from white guys?" I said.

PeeWee shook his head. "Beats me."

❖ ❖ ❖

Three days later Leroy took us back to Cat Island. We walked through the jungle to the dog camp. The Swiss was there with ten handlers and ten dogs. Waiting.

We eyed each other.

None of the handlers looked much older than us in their khaki pants and olive T-shirts.

The dogs were all kinds of breeds, mostly big dogs. When they sat, their heads came up to just below their handlers' waists.

The Swiss walked down the line.

"Shepherd, boxer, bloodhound, pit bull," he said. "Here's your Irish setter, Labrador, and Bouvier. These two are a mix. Some of these animals will be better than others, of course, so we'll be weeding out the timid ones. No one but the handlers will touch, feed, groom, encourage, reward, or command the dogs, is that clear?"

The dogs were on silver choke chains. Each sat quietly on the left side of its handler. Nice, I thought. Handsome animals.

The Swiss assigned ten of us to the ten handlers. "The rest of you follow me," he said.

I got assigned to a handler named Smith. His dog was Kooch, a German shepherd.

Cobra got hooked up with King, a Labrador.

Chik got the Bouvier, Bingo.

Shig got Spit, a pit bull.

My dog was the biggest. He held his head high and looked smart.

Smith seemed about eighteen, nineteen at the most. Hard to tell with haoles. He stood about four inches taller than me, with a head that seemed too small for his body. He didn't look ugly, just different. He had a canvas bag slung over one shoulder and didn't offer to shake hands.

His dog, Kooch, gazed at me and wagged his tail. I couldn't help smiling—somebody's pet, like Leroy said, volunteered to serve in the army.

"Hey, boy," I said, forgetting what the Swiss had just told us. I stuck out my hand for Kooch to smell.

Smith jerked back on the choke chain. "Don't touch or speak to the dog."

"Sorry."

"Follow me."

Smith and Kooch headed into the trees.

The other handlers each took a separate path.

Ten minutes later Smith stopped in a clearing. He sat on a fallen tree and motioned for me to find a spot myself.

"Don't mind that old Swiss guy," he said. "He sounds grumpy, but he's not as bad as he seems. What's your name?"

"Eddy Okubo, sir."

"You don't have to call me sir. Just Smith."

"Okay . . . Smith."

"Now listen, Kubo. The first and most important thing you need to know is what the old man said—this dog is not your pet. He's not my pet, either, but we have a certain relationship."

Smith ran his hand over Kooch's head.

The dog panted in the heat.

"He's a war dog. And that's a different kind of animal than somebody's house dog. He answers to me and only me. So get any notion you have about making friends with him out of your head. That's just not in the cards. Understood?"

"Understood."

Smith studied me long enough to satisfy himself that I got it.

"What are all those other dogs doing?" I asked, thinking of the hundreds of kennels I saw. "I mean, we not going work with all of them, right?"

"No, we've got all kinds of work going on here. What you're doing is just part of it."

I nodded. "All these dogs were somebody's pets?"

"Sure were. You know, most people think that if they have a vicious dog, he would be perfect for this kind of duty. But it's the exact opposite. What you want is a dog that obeys. You got to have some aggressiveness, sure, but it's more important to have an animal that will do exactly what you tell him to do. And he has to have a keen sense of smell and hearing. You want smart, not vicious."

Made sense to me.

Smith put his hands on his knees and pushed himself to his feet. "So let's get started."

I heard voices not far off and glanced through the trees. Cobra and his handler were hiking parallel to us. I wondered how he was going to do this, because he hadn't settled with the dog bait idea like I had. But worse for him was that he didn't like dogs—unless they were tied up or behind some-body's fence. I grinned. A little rat dog like Sharky would probably seem pretty good to him right now.

Smith heard the voices, too, and headed away until we couldn't see or hear anyone else.

Finally, he stopped.

"All right, in a minute I'm going to send you off into the trees here."

He glanced back to be sure no one else was nearby. "Everyone's doing the same exercise today, so we have to get some distance between us."

Kooch stood patiently.

"Now, you . . . what's your name again?"

"Eddy Okubo."

"Right. Okay, Kubo. You need to watch out for a few things on this island. First, we got some nasty snakes—cop-perheads, cottonmouths, and coral snakes. All poisonous, all deadly. I'll point them out if we see them. The important thing is that if you spot one, give it plenty of room. We got some stuff for snakebites, but believe me, you don't want to get bit. Watch for gators, too. They pretty much don't want to be anywhere near you, but if you stumble onto one of 'em you might find yourself in a heap of trouble. I once saw a man get his leg took off by one. There's also boars, and they're dangerous, too, but we don't see those too much. And deer, but they ain't nothing to worry about. I seen a scorpion once or twice," Smith said, wincing. "Man, I *hate* those things!"

Smith was a talker, all right.

I glanced around the jungle. It was hard to imagine that so many dangerous creatures could be on such a small island.

"So, here's the plan for today, Kubo. And probably for the next week or so. Depends on when the dog gets it. Some learn faster than others. Personally, I think the shepherd is the best breed we got in the K-9 Corps. So we're kind of lucky, you and me."

He glanced down and rubbed Kooch's head. "Yeah. You're a smart dog, ain't ya, boy?"

Kooch looked up at Smith, his tongue dripping.

"Lucky dog, too," Smith added.

"How come lucky?"

Smith hesitated.

"You heard of a suicide dog?"

I shook my head.

"Well, it's kind of hush-hush, but they're training those here, too. Boxers, mostly. What they are is dogs with explosives tied to their necks. They train them to leap into dugouts and foxholes. The explosives are set off by radio."

"They blow up the *dog*?"

"Uh-huh."

"But . . ."

Smith shook his head. "This is war."

We sat in silence, thinking.

Smith sighed and reached into the canvas bag. He pulled out a jar. It was packed with something wet and red. He held it up and gazed into it, gleaming in the sunlight.

He tossed me the jar.

Looked like guts. "What is it?"

"Horsemeat in blood and water."

He pulled a coil of string out of his bag. "That meat is for the scent."

"Scent?"

"Uh-huh. Kooch's going to get a whiff of what's in that jar—and he'll want to eat it, but you're not going to give it to him. Not yet, anyway. You take a piece of meat out and tie it to this string. Then you drag it into the trees. Me and the dog will stay back here awhile and give you a chance to find a place to hide—not too close, now—go off a ways. Then he's going to find you."

"That's it?"

"The minute he alerts me to where you are, I'm going to fire a shot with a small air gun. When you hear that shot, I want you to fall down, lie on your back, take the rest of that meat out of the jar, and put it on your throat. The dog's going to come up and eat it off you, right there under your chin."

29
HORSEMEAT

Smith tossed me his pocketknife. I cut off a small piece of meat, raw and smelly, and tied it to the string. When I handed the knife back, Smith ran both sides of the blade along his pants leg before folding it back into the handle.

Kooch's eyes never left the raw meat. He rose to his feet when I unscrewed the lid. I let him sniff inside the jar. He tried to snap the meat up.

Smith jerked back on the leash.

I put the lid back on the jar.

Smith took off the choke chain and replaced it with a leather collar. "When this collar goes on, he knows he's going to work. At least, that's what I'm trying to get through to him."

"Looks like a smart dog," I said.

Smith eyed me, as if something about me didn't quite fit.

"How old are you, anyway?" he said. "You look kind of scrawny."

"Uh . . . eighteen," I mumbled.

Smith humphed. "Not a chance. I'm eighteen, and you ain't that. My guess is sixteen—seventeen at the most."

I glanced back over my shoulder, pretending I'd heard something.

"Hey, it don't matter to me, Kubo. Not for a minute. So go ahead and take off. Go out as far as you can. Hide somewhere. The dog's going to hunt you down. Don't forget about the horsemeat, now—when he finds you, lie down and put it on your throat like I said. Understand?"

I nodded.

"I'll give you a ten-minute lead. Go!"

I dragged the hunk of meat into the trees, keeping away from rotting logs and those quiet ponds. Alligators and snakes snapped and slithered in my head. I had to find out where those things hid. I'd never seen a snake in my life, but that was about to change. At least I had boots on, and now I knew why.

I heard a shout far away. Cobra? Chik? Maybe they had raw horsemeat on their throats right now. That was so weird—a dog eating raw meat off your neck.

But it was what the army wanted.

I stumbled over a fallen tree and found a carved-out sandy trench behind it. I could get down under it and hide.

I glanced back and saw only the motionless jungle. I found a stick, then poked it under the tree, rocking the trunk with my foot. When no snakes or scorpions flew out, I crouched under it and waited.

Stillness surrounded me.

No sounds, no breeze. All those dogs running around looking for us, and not one bark. That was something, how they worked so quietly.

Five minutes passed.

Ants, a motionless lizard, white clouds hanging in the sky. Shadows on my arm.

I peeked up over the tree. Not even a bird or a dragonfly. I loosened the lid and set the open jar of horsemeat on the sand.

Ten minutes later I heard a quiet snap. I peeked over the tree.

Kooch and Smith—the dog's nose roaming the exact same ground I had stepped on.

Kooch sniffed more frantically now, sweeping the sand, inching silently closer.

He stopped, head up, alerting Smith with two raised ears. Not one growl, not even a whimper.

I stood like Smith said, and Smith shot his air gun.

I fell as if shot, and quickly scooped out the slimy meat and held it dripping watery blood on my neck.

Within seconds Kooch's big wet nose was inches from mine. One swallowing gulp and the meat was gone. He licked my neck and my face.

"You like that, huh?" I whispered, rubbing his ears. "Yeah, you a good dog."

Smith ran up and leashed Kooch, stroking him and praising him.

I sat up and rubbed sand between my hands to get rid of the stink. It didn't work.

Smith pulled another jar out of his bag and tossed it to me. "Let's do it again."

I caught it and stood up, brushing the sand off my pants. "He didn't even bark."

"Trained that way. You want the dog to alert you to the enemy, not the other way around."

Kooch sat just beside Smith's left foot, panting. "He's good," I said. "He found me easy."

"He'll be finding you Japs without meat in no time."

I glanced away when he said "Japs." *What are you haoles, stupid? Don't you know that's insulting?*

"He can find me because of the meat," I said. "That don't mean he can tell a Japanese from anyone else."

"Franz says he can."

"I don't believe it."

"Why not?"

"You think we smell diff'rent from you?"

Smith gave me a curious look. "Well, don't you?"

"I don't see why we would."

Smith nodded. Then he grinned. "Guess we'll find out, huh?"

30
THE SCENT

After Kooch ate the second hunk of meat off my neck, I found a rust-colored pond to wash up in—of course, me and Smith checked it out for alligators first. What we didn't see was the water moccasin racing toward us.

"Jeese!" Smith yelped, leaping back as I sprinted for the trees.

But it veered away from us and slithered into the weeds. It was the first snake I'd ever seen, and it was in the *water*.

"Dang things," Smith said. "Lucky for us he ran away like you did." He shuddered. "Go ahead. You can wash up now."

I inched back to the water and quickly cleaned my hands.

"You can sometimes see alligator eyes poking up in the water," Smith said. "Look like two lumps. And they hide along the shore, too, just like that snake. Sometimes you

141

never know they're in there until they explode up and scare the living daylights out of you—could be they might come after you, too, if you get them mad. So never forget to check first. You don't want to be surprised by *anything* in this place."

I scrubbed as Smith went on. The smell of blood didn't want to come off my hands.

"We'll do this horsemeat thing a few more times over the next week or so," Smith said. "Then we'll move on to the real stuff."

I sat back on my heels. "Huh?"

"I'll watch out for you, Kubo. Relax."

✢ ✢ ✢

That afternoon we met up with the rest of the guys back in the clearing. The handlers and their dogs went their way, and we went back to the boat.

"Did you do the horsemeat thing?" Cobra asked.

"Yeah, can you believe it?"

"I can't get the stink off my hands."

"Check out mines," Chik said, sticking his fingers in Cobra's face.

Cobra batted him away. "*Bakatare!* You prob'ly ate that meat yourself, ah?"

Chik laughed. "Yum. Ate it raw, like a man."

"You sick," Cobra spat.

"If this is war, give me more," Chik said, wagging his eyebrows.

The *Sugar Babe* was sleeping in the water right where

we'd left it. And so was Leroy. All you could see of him were his dirty socks, resting up on the gunnel. We took off our boots and waded out. Felt good on my hot and sweaty feet.

"Hey, Leroy," Shig called. "You still alive?"

The socks moved. Leroy's head popped up. He squinted and rubbed a hand over his face. "How long I been asleep?" he said, yawning.

"Too long," Cobra said. "Take us home."

Leroy dragged himself up and scratched his belly, then went to the wheel and fired up the engine as we climbed aboard.

Cat Island shrank behind us, quiet and mysterious. "Cobra," I said. "You think we smell diff'rent from white guys?"

"I hope so," he said, shifting his eyes toward Leroy.

"No, really. You think we smell diff'rent?"

"Nope."

"It's crazy."

"Going get worse."

I frowned and turned away. So far only bad things happened, and always just when it was getting good. For a while at Camp McCoy I'd thought we would be treated like real soldiers.

But no. Not us.

31
PICKET BOATS

Halfway back to Ship Island, *Sugar Babe*'s engine coughed up some black smoke.

And died.

Leroy tried to start it back up again, but it wouldn't kick over. "Dang," he said, then ducked down to the engine room.

The breeze was strong and getting stronger. *Sugar Babe* rolled side to side, the wrinkled gulf waters spanking the hull.

Ten minutes later Leroy poked his head up. "Anybody here a mechanic?"

We shook our heads, a few faces turning green from the rolling boat.

"I know a little bit," I said, when nobody else spoke up. "My pop builds boats like this."

"Well, hot dang, son, get yourself on down here, then."

The engine room was some stink place. A half inch of dirty bilgewater mixed with oil and diesel fuel sloshed around my feet, the smell musty and sickening if you weren't used to it.

Leroy swept his hand over the gray-painted engine. "Take a look-see. I sure can't figure it out." Sweat dripped off his forehead. He wiped it away with his thumb.

I backed off. Between Leroy's smell and the bilgewater I didn't know how long I could stay down there.

I studied the engine.

Seemed strange to me that Leroy made a living with his boat and didn't know how to fix it when it broke down.

The gulf grew choppier, the wind starting to blow us toward Mexico. We were too far out to swim to Cat or Ship. If we couldn't fix it, we'd have to radio for help.

"I don't see anything that stands out," I said. "Could be a clogged fuel line, or maybe the fuel pump. Don't really know, though."

"Piece of junk!" Leroy spat. "Good-fer-nothing piece of floating dry rot."

Back up on deck I took deep, thirsty breaths of the breeze, a sweet-smelling kiss from heaven.

By now night was coming on. We'd been stuck there for close to an hour.

"Better break out the radio and get some help," I said.

Leroy shook his head. "Ain't got one."

"You got a boat with no *radio*?" Cobra said.

"I got a radio, but it's t'home."

Cobra gaped.

"It had some problems," Leroy said, opening his hands. "I was working on it."

"How loud can you yell?" Shig said.

But it wasn't funny, because the two islands were fading away.

Leroy went back down to the engine room. We sat silently on the moving water, with the sound of Leroy's wrench clanking up the companionway.

In the west, the sun sank red into the wind-torn sea. The sky and water began to darken.

An hour later all daylight was gone.

Leroy gave up, came back, and rattled through a drawer for his flashlight. The battery leaked rusty acid. In a small hold he found a flare gun. With one flare.

He grinned. "This ought to get someone's attention."

"If it works," Cobra mumbled.

"Stand back." Leroy held the flare gun high, ducking his head as if the thing might backfire on him.

Foonk!

The flare rocketed straight up, then arched over and fell slowly, parachuting into the sea. But we were a long way from anyone who might see it.

The small glowing ball poofed out when it hit water, just like the fire on Pop's sampan when it sank.

Back to full dark. Stars coming out.

"Let's just hope someone saw that," Leroy said. "Or else tomorrow we might end up on some beach drinking Mexican beer." He laughed, a small nervous sound that turned into a cough.

We sat rocking on the water.

146

Leroy went back down to work on the engine by the light of a gas lantern that made me nervous, it was so fumy down there.

PeeWee staggered over to the gunnel and leaned over the side. He didn't throw up, but he was close. And he wasn't the only one.

"We got to get back to dry land," Chik said. "I starting to taste copper."

"Shhh," Cobra said. "Listen."

Engines—a low grumbling.

Small boat lights, vague in the blackness.

"Hey, Leroy," Shig called. "Someone saw that flare."

Leroy came bounding up the companionway with the lantern. He stretched up to peer into the darkness. "Praise the Lord," he said, waving the lantern back and forth above his head.

Chik groaned and bent over.

"Don't toss it in the boat," Cobra said.

PeeWee sat back down, cradling his gut.

When the approaching boat was almost on us, a bright white searchlight burst to life, catching us like roaches. I shielded my eyes with my hand.

A U.S. Coast Guard picket boat, about twice the size of the *Sugar Babe,* throttled down and sat idling on our starboard side.

"Engine broke down," Leroy called over to them, squinting into the brilliant white light. "Mind turning that thing off? We could use a tow."

The light moved away, shooting into the water nearby, but it stayed on. Now we could see the picket boat—and the four men with rifles standing on deck, aiming our way. "Stand by," someone called.

"We'll see if we can do that," Leroy mumbled. "Jeese."

Nothing happened.

The guys with the rifles never took their eyes off us.

"Hey," Leroy called again. "What's the matter? We need a tow."

"I said to stand by."

"For what?"

There was no response.

"Good Lord almighty." Leroy shook his head.

PeeWee groaned. He staggered up and dove for the gunnel.

Bam! Bam! Bam!

Water spouted up as bullets thwacked into the side of the *Sugar Babe*. We hit the deck. PeeWee fell back into the boat with blood dripping down his face and a splinter the size of a pencil stuck in his cheek.

"No, no, no!" Leroy shouted, holding his hands above his head. "Stop! Don't shoot!"

"Hold your fire!" someone yelled on the picket boat.

We got up and hunched around PeeWee. "Ahhh," he groaned. The splinter was stabbed all the way through his cheek into his mouth.

"Good God," Leroy gasped. "What'd you shoot for?" he shouted. "These men are soldiers in the U.S. Army!"

I tore off my T-shirt and held it up to PeeWee's cheek to stop the blood, careful not to touch the splinter. "Hang on," I said. "We'll get that thing out." He was lucky it wasn't a bullet, or half his face would have disappeared.

Leroy sprang toward the companionway, his hands up so he wouldn't get shot. "I'm getting the first-aid kit," he yelled to the guys on the picket boat.

North of us, coming from Gulfport or Biloxi, more lights raced our way.

Leroy came back and fumbled out a bottle of hydrogen peroxide. He opened it with trembling fingers and poured half of it on PeeWee's wound. It bubbled up pink.

"Uhhhgh," PeeWee gasped.

I ripped off my belt and folded it over. "Bite this," I said, sticking it between his teeth. "I going pull that thing out of your cheek."

PeeWee bit down on the belt and squeezed his eyes tight. Slowly, I pulled the splinter out.

Cobra covered the hole with the T-shirt, now sopped with hydrogen peroxide. PeeWee spat the belt out. "Ahh, that hurts," he squeaked.

When I looked up there were three picket boats surrounding us.

"You men hold your dang fire over there," Leroy shouted.

Now Shig and Ricky had to throw up—they eased slowly to the gunnel, hands up for the rifle guys to see.

Finally, one of the picket boats maneuvered closer. "Heads up," someone called.

Out of the blackness a loop of rope thumped on deck.

Leroy grabbed it and walked it forward to the bow. "What's the problem? Why you so trigger-happy?"

"No problem."

"What do you mean, no problem? This kid is wounded!

You've scared us half to death, and we've been waiting for over an hour. You call that no problem?"

The coast guard guy said, "You want a tow or not?"

Leroy shut up.

✣ ✣ ✣

That night back in the barrack Ricky Kondo patched up PeeWee's face with gauze and tape. PeeWee could have used stitches, but he wasn't about to let Ricky stick him with a needle and thread.

We were all eerily quiet.

Because somebody could have died.

Maybe all of us.

✣ ✣ ✣

Two days later, Leroy came back to Ship Island with the *Sugar Babe* running like a top. He was glad to see PeeWee up to his old self so quickly. "They got to give you a Purple Heart, son," he said as he examined the bandage on PeeWee's cheek. "Only I wonder if they do that when you get wounded by your own guys."

PeeWee grinned and said, "You play five-card stud, Leroy?"

"Are you kidding? Ain't nobody better."

PeeWee wagged his eyebrows. "Come early sometime, we get a game up."

"Hah! Good to see you doing so well," Leroy said, tapping PeeWee's shoulder.

"So what was wrong with the boat?" I said.

"Fuel pump, like you thought. I had the army buy me a new one—and a radio." Leroy grinned. "Found out why they made us wait, too. They thought they'd captured the whole Jap navy. Seems not even the coast guard knows about you army dog guys. They took us for saboteurs."

Leroy thought a moment. "I guess I'da figured that, too, if I was in their shoes."

32
THE
SLINGSHOT

For another week, Smith had me dragging horsemeat through the jungles of Cat Island. I got to know my way around pretty well.

"Make it harder," he said. "Hide like your life depends on it. Think of the dog as capable of ripping your throat out and causing you to bleed to death. Where would you hide then? Use your imagination."

Man, I thought. Ripping my throat out? Where am I, in somebody's nightmare?

I hid in swampy bayous. I climbed up into trees. I hid up-wind, behind a bushy rise. I lay flat and covered myself with leaves and sand.

Kooch found me every time.

Smith made a change. "Take off your T-shirt and drag

that," he said. "I want him on *your* scent, now. But he's still going to eat the meat off your throat, okay?"

"Sure."

Kooch had such a good nose, it was impossible to fool him. Each time he found me I put the slimy meat on my throat, and as always, he'd savage it down, then lick my neck and face, almost like kissing me. And I'd whisper to him quick, before Smith ran up. "Hey, boy, you a good dog, yeah."

But one time Smith heard me.

"Hey!" he shouted. "I told you not to make friends with him."

"I'm not. I'm doing what you said. I can't help it if he likes me."

"Oh yes you can."

He poked around in his backpack and came up with a slingshot. He tested the rubber, then flung it at me.

"He's too friendly. That has to change. If it doesn't, then everything we're doing here won't be worth spit. Now, let's do this again. After he finds you and eats the meat, you put something in that slingshot and shoot it at him. Hurt him. Chase him away."

I stared at Smith. "I . . . I can't do that."

"What?"

"You want me to hurt Kooch?"

"That's what I just said, isn't it?"

I studied Smith's eyes, the slingshot dangling from my fingers.

Smith tossed me another jar of horsemeat. "Take off," he said.

Fine.

At first, I hid in a tree. If I was up there, Kooch couldn't lick me, so I wouldn't have to shoot him with the slingshot. But that wasn't what Smith wanted.

I jumped down and squatted in a stand of thick marsh grass at the edge of a dark-water pond—after I'd poked a stick into it. In the mud I found five marble-sized stones. I jammed four of them into my pocket. The fifth went into the slingshot's leather webbing.

Kooch found me. Smith shot his air gun, and I fell back in the muddy grass. Kooch ran up and ate the meat off my throat. When he started to lick up the extra blood and water, I rolled away and drew the slingshot taut. I aimed at his hindquarters, where it would sting, but not hurt him.

My fingers trembled, the webbing wobbling in my hand.

I couldn't do it.

I could hear Smith running up behind me. "Shoot him!" he shouted. "What are you waiting for?"

Kooch yelped when the stone hit, and scurried off. He looked back, standing sideways, like saying, Hey, what'd you do that for?

"Hit him again," Smith ordered.

Kooch yipped and jumped when my second shot hit his hip. But this time he growled and paced, his head low and the hair on his back prickled up. Keeping his distance.

I couldn't look him in the eye.

"Stand down," Smith said.

I hid the slingshot from Kooch.

Smith called him back and leashed him. He ran his hand down Kooch's neck.

But the dog kept his eyes on me.

"Let's do this one more time, Kubo," Smith said softly.

I hid.

Kooch found me.

I shot him with a stone.

And the whole thing made me sick.

33
TRAINED
TO HATE

Late one morning a few days later, we were on the boat heading over to Cat Island. Dark clouds were stacked up on the horizon in the southeast, smudging the line between sky and water.

"Don't like the look of that," Leroy said.

Cobra sniffed the air. "Storm coming."

"Maybe. But sometimes they veer off and go south."

Cat Island came up off our port side, long and low. I'd come to like it, so rich with life.

"What're y'all doing over there in that jungle, anyway?" Leroy asked, swinging the boat in.

"You don't know?" I said.

Leroy humphed. "They don't tell me squat. Just when to pick y'alls up and to bring your mail when you got any."

Was it okay to tell him? Probably not, or he'd already know.

"We teaching dogs to hate us," Chik said, not even thinking about it.

Leroy gaped. "Say again?"

Chik started to say more, but Ricky Kondo stopped him with a slight shake of his head.

Chik shrugged and fell silent.

Leroy let us off with the cow rays. We waded ashore.

"Keep an eye on the weather," Leroy called. "If it starts to get worse, y'all get back here quick as a wink so I can get you over to Ship and make it home my own self, you hear?"

"Right," Ricky Kondo said.

The wind started to pick up some as we headed inland, enough to rattle the trees and rustle the long grasses. But the clouds were far to the east, and the sun still painted sharp shadows over the sandy trail.

The dogs were lying in the shade, each chained to a separate tree. Their handlers lounged around in a group a short distance behind them.

The dogs turned to look our way as we approached, but they didn't stand.

We stopped in the clearing.

The handlers stayed where they were, didn't come to greet us like usual.

Strange.

"What's going on?" PeeWee whispered.

I spat in the sand. Yeah, what?

Just past the handlers, two guys were working with a

monster Irish wolfhound and a wooden dummy dressed in a Japanese army uniform. The dummy had a gap in its neck, where one guy was securing a hunk of horsemeat. The other guy stood with the wolfhound at his side. When the guy by the dummy got out of the way, the handler turned the wolfhound loose, shouting, *"Kill! Kill!"* and that huge dog flew straight for the throat. *Bam!* Flattened the dummy, ripped the meat out of the throat, and ate it.

"Jeese," Chik said. "That's creepy."

Something was changing—the mood, the way the handlers just stood there.

The two wolfhound guys started setting up the dummy again.

A few minutes later, the Swiss showed up carrying a bundle of empty burlap sacks. He dropped them at our feet. "Grab one, boys. Today, we agitate the dogs."

Agitate?

I picked up a sack, rough and scratchy.

"Our purpose today is to start establishing you boys as the enemy," the Swiss said.

He looked back at the two lines of dogs, all ten now standing ready. He nodded, and the handlers moved out to check the chains, test their strength.

The Swiss turned back to us. "Form a line."

Shig was first. PeeWee, Cobra, me, and a line of guys behind me.

"Before we begin today's fieldwork, we're going to warm the dogs up, so to speak. I'm going to have you walk down the path between them, right down the middle, and when you do you'll slap at them with those sacks until they raise their lips and bare their teeth."

Got to be kidding, I thought.

"Don't hold back. You are the enemy from here on out. They must know that."

I waited for him to grin and say, Nah, just joking.

He motioned to Shig. "Come on, let's go!"

Shig glanced back at the rest of us, then slowly walked toward the line of dogs, trailing the sack like a whip.

He raised his arm. Then dropped it and looked at the Swiss. I rubbed Herbie's blue stone in my pocket, worrying for Shig.

"Go ahead," the Swiss said. "Hit them."

Shig pressed his lips tight and started in on the first dog—King, Cobra's Labrador.

At first King thought it was a game and tried to grab the sack and tug on it. "Hit him harder," the Swiss called. "But not near the eyes, don't hit the eyes."

Shig whapped the dog with increasing force.

The reaction was quick and terrifying.

Shig staggered back at King's raised lips and ugly snarl, deep, from way down inside. Shig quickly moved on to the next dog, and the next, each one leaping at him violently when he struck with the sack, trying to bite him. Only the chains yanked them back.

"Make them *feel* it," the Swiss shouted, motioning for the rest of us to get moving. "Let's go! Let's go!"

We followed Shig like we were going to a funeral. Reluctantly, I wrapped the burlap around my fist.

I hit King weakly, faking it. I went after the next dog, and one more, slapping them lightly. To hit them any harder was impossible. How could I be doing such a thing?

Ahead, Kooch was snarling at Cobra, and Cobra was keeping his distance, whipping the sack at him, but barely close enough to hit.

Smith watched, his squinted face thin-lipped, his hands balled into fists. He hated this as much as I did.

"Move in! Get closer!" the Swiss shouted.

When I came to Kooch I whipped the burlap at his side. I hoped he'd recognize me and understand I was only doing this because I had to. But I knew dogs didn't think that way. A threat was a threat. Period. And Kooch was way too worked up by then; he had to defend himself.

Kooch lunged.

His yellowish teeth looked like sharpened bones. He snarled so hard he almost choked. This wasn't the dog I knew. Days earlier he'd been kissing my face. Now he wanted to kill.

Me.

"Hurt him!" the Swiss shouted.

I struck harder, trying to keep the burlap from his eyes. Kooch snagged the sack and pulled on it, shaking his head, the noise in him rising from some deep place a thousand years old.

I jerked until I got the sack back and quickly moved on to the next dog, a collie named Captain. My hands shook. My lip bled where I'd been biting on it.

Suddenly, my mind flipped off, replaced by a merciful blankness as I moved through the line of raging dogs. Don't think, don't think, don't think.

160

By the time the last of us had come through the line, the dogs were worked into a frenzy, all ten of them leaping, drooling, half insane. If a chain broke, someone would pay.

"Start over," the Swiss ordered. "Let's go!"

The wind was starting to bend the treetops. A high layer of white clouds rolled west, blocking the sun.

Four times we beat the dogs with the sacks, and all the while the handlers watched unmoving from the shadows. Only when the dogs began to grow hoarse did the Swiss call us off.

I was cold with sweat, my hands raw from the sandpapery burlap.

"That was good work," he said. "I know you didn't like it, but you did well."

He glanced up at the swaying trees. "I think the weather is about to change for the worse. You'd better get back to your boat. Next time we do this it will be more dangerous. You'll have protection, of course, but it's never really safe. Remember always that the dog is made to fight and to kill. Mercy is not in him when he's in battle. To him it's win or lose. There's no middle ground."

On the way back to the boat, the wind grew stronger. The sky darkened and the light began to fail. The *Sugar Babe* bobbed on the water where we'd left it, with whitecaps like shattered glass tossed over the gulf beyond.

Leroy stood with legs spread on the bow, motioning for us to hurry up. He cupped his hands around his mouth and shouted, but the wind stole the words right out of his mouth.

34
GUTS

Through the night the winds howled in the sea grass, rattling the windows of our creaky barrack. The few minutes I did manage to sleep were mangled by dreams of whips and snarling dogs. My sweaty sheets were twisted up like rope when dawn finally broke.

And still, the wind screamed and the windows rattled.

Amazingly, the supply boat showed up.

That skipper has a stomach of steel, I thought.

Seven of us ran out to meet him at the pier. We leaned into the wind, hands up to protect our faces against the fine grains of sand that hit like flying pins.

But the skipper refused to dock. He stood a ways out, appearing and disappearing in the rise and fall of the sea swells.

He waved, motioning for us to go around to the other side of the island, where the wind might be less fierce. He'd get the supplies to us there.

"But how?" Shig said. "No pier there."

"I think he wants us to row out to him," Ricky Kondo said. "Shig, Cobra, Eddy, grab a rowboat. Carry it low so the wind won't yank it out of your hands. James, dig up some oars."

The sea was more manageable on the south side.

Barely.

The supply boat clawed its way around the point and hove to about fifty yards out. We carried the rowboat into the water and launched it. "I'll row it out," James said, rolling over into it. We gave him a shove.

He took some slams when the waves hit, but he made it through without capsizing. When he reached the supply boat, he turned and raised his arms. We cheered, then watched the skipper lower box after box of supplies, while James secured them in the rowboat.

When the supplies were loaded, James started back to shore. But now the rowboat was heavy. He had muscle, for sure, and he was truly an able-bodied seaman—but the wind blew him back, farther and farther away from the supply boat, and away from shore.

"He not going make it," Shig shouted over the wind.

"Hey!" Cobra yelled, motioning to the skipper. "He needs help!"

But the skipper didn't respond.

"He's not going to do anything," Ricky Kondo said.

We stood gawking. James hunched over the oars, going to Mexico . . . or to the bottom of the sea.

Slim ripped off his shirt and pants and ran into the cold water, ducking under the jagged waves and popping up on the back side.

He was the best swimmer of all of us, and reached the rowboat quickly, the wind at his back. James helped him aboard, the rowboat rising and falling, rising and falling.

They took turns rowing.

When the supply boat skipper saw that they were making headway back to the island, he throttled up and got out of there.

Waves battered the rowboat, nearly tipping it over a time or two. But Slim and James fought back.

We waded out as far as we could to help.

When we finally got our hands on the skiff, Slim slumped over the oars, unable to lift his weakened arms. James could barely dig out the bow line.

"We got it from here," Cobra said. "You okay?"

"Fine," James said, "but Slim needs a blanket, fast. He's turning blue."

Slim stumbled out of the boat, shivering. Cobra helped him back to the barrack and got some hot water going. The rest of us took care of the supplies and the rowboat.

An hour later, we all fell onto our cots, blanketed in warmth, the woodstove snapping.

Slim slept the rest of that afternoon. What he'd done was the bravest thing I'd seen in the army so far. He could have drowned. He could've gone down with hypothermia.

Later that evening, with the wind still howling outside, I said, "What made you do it?"

Slim shrugged. "It was nothing. Any one of us would have done it. Anyway, we couldn't let James drift to Mexico and have all the fun, ah?"

James grinned. "Ay, chihuahua."

A great gust whoomped against the barrack and rattled the windows. Cobra glanced at the exposed rafters. "We going lose this roof if this don't let up soon."

"Man, I sure hope this don't turn into a hurricane," Chik said.

Shig waved him off. "No worry, Chickaboom. If that happens, we just go inside that fort."

We all nodded. Yeah, the fort's been here since old times, it will be here when the storm is over.

It was hard to sleep that night, thinking about hurricanes and waves washing over the island, the kind of thoughts that loom like red-eyed demons in the blackness of night.

✤ ✤ ✤

Morning came with a heavy, steel gray sky. The ocean was rough, but the storm had definitely moved on.

Leroy didn't show.

Not for four more days.

So we went fishing and wrote letters. It was peaceful. And boring. Chik's nervous leg was bouncing all over the place. You could hear music inside him again, like the old days in Kaka'ako.

But all during that time I kept thinking about Slim, and how he hadn't even thought twice about helping James. We were supposed to be fighting for our country in this army, in this war. But here on this island we had to look out for ourselves, because for sure nobody else was.

35
THE ENEMY

When Leroy finally returned, I still wasn't ready. I would have done anything to get out of hitting those dogs again.

Anything.

Back on Cat Island, we slogged ashore and headed into the jungle. No chatter. Not a word. Even Chik was off in his head somewhere.

I stared at my feet as I walked, not thinking about snakes or alligators or anything else—only those burlap sacks.

Just before we got to the clearing, we stopped.

We couldn't even look at each other.

Ricky Kondo gave us a minute, then nodded.

The dogs jumped to their feet when we came into view. They knew us now. The enemy.

The Swiss came out of a large tent holding a steaming

cup. "This way," he said, motioning for us to walk toward him between the chained dogs.

We inched ahead. The dogs watched us, ears perked. Ready.

I tried not to look at them.

But that was impossible.

As we got closer, they started lunging and snapping their chains taut, straining, snarling, ready to rip through our thin pants and T-shirts. We no longer needed the burlap sacks.

In those dogs there wasn't even a trace of the family pets they used to be.

The Swiss took a sip from his cup, then nodded. "Good. We're ready to move on."

✛ ✛ ✛

Smith took me deep into the jungle.

Kooch kept a suspicious eye on me, but he seemed to have cooled his fire. He followed Smith, keeping to the left side.

We stopped at a small opening in the trees.

"Set here a minute," Smith said.

We both eased down cross-legged on the sand. Kooch settled next to Smith, panting. Just being a dog.

Smith picked up a handful of sand and let it slip through his fingers.

Then he looked up.

"What we're going to do today will be about as much fun as sticking your fist into a meat grinder, so pay attention— always, from now on, pay attention. This dog will rip you to shreds if you're not careful."

Kooch stopped panting and looked off into the trees, hearing something no human could. A moment later, he relaxed and settled back down.

"You've got to know something important," Smith went on, "and that is that a good dog—like Kooch here—when they fight, they fight to the end. They don't give in and they don't give up. He'll show you no mercy if he's mad enough. That's the way these animals are made."

I winced, because I knew Smith was right. After whipping those dogs, what I needed now was a steel cage to hide in.

"If for some reason you fall or stumble, and I can't stop him, kneel over on the ground with your arms covering your head. If he gets to your neck it's all over. Do you understand that?"

I nodded, putting a hand to my throat.

"We got to do it this way. That's how this dog will learn to be the dog he has to be. He's going to be so well trained that no jungle Jap will ever sleep at night."

I waited, my eyes down.

"I'm not going to let him hurt you, okay?"

I looked up, squinting. "That would be good."

We stared at each other.

"All right," he said. "We're going to start with the burlap sack and work our way up to the sleeve."

"What's that?"

"Padding. You'll see. Just remember, this is dead serious work. You can't get complacent about any of it, so keep alert and stay ready."

Smith stood and pulled a burlap sack out of his canvas

bag and tossed it to me. "Knot up one end and grab it good and tight."

I got up, knotted the sack, and gripped it like a whip.

Kooch stopped panting and clamped his jaw, his eyes on that sack. The hair on the back of his neck started to bristle.

"Hide the burlap on your far side," Smith said. "It's what he perceives as the threat . . . for now."

I quickly hid it behind me.

That seemed to settle Kooch. A little. But when I raised it a hair, he became instantly alert.

Smith switched to the leather collar.

Kooch got up and stood at Smith's side, never taking his eyes off me.

"Okay," Smith said. "Dig in. Spread your feet apart and bend your knees. Left side toward me, the sack out of view."

I got into position, ready as I could be, and glanced around for a tree I could run to if I needed to climb for my life. They were everywhere, but Kooch would be on me before I took two steps.

"All right, here's the plan. I want the dog thinking about *you* now, not the sack. It's all about you, the enemy. And we need to build his confidence by making you appear smaller. We want him to believe that even though you are a threat to him, you are fearful of him."

That won't be hard, I thought.

It was easy enough to look fearful, but I couldn't *be* fearful, because if I was, and I did things wrong, I would get hurt.

Sweat rolled down my neck.

"Now, keeping that sack out of sight, I want you to back

170

away into the trees. Wait there a minute, then come out. And when you do, you will be the enemy. Remember that. You're a Jap on some Pacific island, slinking around and trying to find and kill a U.S. soldier. Got that?"

I got it, all right. A Jap.

"You ever meet my CO, Smith?"

"What?"

"Major Parrish, you ever meet him?"

"Nope."

"You should. He has a way that don't rub you wrong."

Smith narrowed his eyes. "What's that supposed to mean?"

"He don't call us Japs."

"Listen, you . . ."

Before he could finish I backed into the trees.

When I couldn't see Smith, I stopped and waited, trying to calm down.

Through the leaves I could see Smith studying his feet and rubbing the back of his neck.

"All right," he called, looking up. "Come out mean. Slink like a killer. Make a face only a mother could love, but don't look directly at the dog until I say so. As far as he can tell, you haven't noticed him yet."

I took a deep breath, then crept out into the open, the sack hidden. To look mean I thought about the centipede boys on Coral Street in Kaka'ako. I knew how to make their stink looks. Yeah, I could do that.

Out of the corner of my eye I could see Kooch drop his head low.

"He's just seen you," Smith said. "Now turn toward him

and freeze. And show him that you're scared of him. Remember, we're building his confidence."

I stopped and stared at Kooch, then crouched and stepped backward.

"Okay, come forward again, slowly. If he leaps at you, back off. But come in again. Back off every time he challenges you, but keep on returning, closer and closer."

I moved ahead.

Kooch growled. He jumped, jerking Smith forward.

I flew back.

Then came in again.

Kooch lunged.

I came back, again and again.

"Don't look at the dog," Smith said. "You're afraid of him, not trying to intimidate him. Okay, good. This time, whip the sack to one side of him, and keep it low."

I bent at the knee and stepped in, bringing the sack around. I snapped it back just as it touched his side.

Kooch went nuts.

I staggered away, my heart about to leap up into my throat.

Smith dug his heels into the sand and pulled back on the leash. "Good, good," he said. "Perfect. Won't be long before he attacks you without that sack, and that's where we're going with this. Let's do it again."

Two hours later, both of us dripping with sweat, Smith raised his hand. "The dog's losing interest. What do you say we call it a day, huh?"

Smith replaced the leather collar with the chain. I kept

away from Kooch, though he didn't seem interested in me anymore.

We headed back through the jungle, Kooch just like somebody's pet again. But now I knew how easily that could change.

And how fast.

For three days, ten of us played the sneaky Jap—that's what Cobra's guy, Burns, called us. Shig, Chik, and Cobra all got dog bites, not bad ones, luckily. But what worried us was that those bites came while the dogs were on their leashes. What if they were ever loose? I asked Smith if that would ever happen.

"We're only getting started, Kubo," he said. "We want them to take you down, and they'll be loose for that, count on it."

Every day when Kooch and I faced each other I thought, This is for you, Pop. I'll do what I promised when I took that oath. The army is not going to crush me. I'll never give up.

36
THE URGE TO KILL

One sweaty hot afternoon I was fishing off the pier with Shig and Cobra. The air was thick and smelled like seaweed.

"You know," I said, "it's funny how one minute my dog don't care about me and the next he's ready to eat me for lunch. Off and on, like a switch. Your dogs like that, too?"

Shig nodded.

Cobra scowled. "We was having a nice, peaceful time. Now I got that in my head."

"Sorry."

"What, Cobra," Shig said. "You not having fun?"

"Sure I'm having fun. You like see my bites? I wear them with pride. And I love it when those dogs show me how they going take my face off when they get loose. Who wouldn't like that? No, what I hate is how we always second-rate to

174

the haoles, ah? We the dog bait, we the targets—not them. Always the Jap, ah?"

Shig and I nodded.

A silent moment went by.

"But we do it anyway," I said.

"Orders," Shig said. "We soldiers. But more important, we Japanese, and no matter which side of this war you on, there ain't no Japanese anywhere going shame himself. That's just us, ah? Good or bad."

Cobra spat. "It's good, every time it's good. But that don't mean I like being second-rate."

"Yeah."

"Yeah."

✣ ✣ ✣

Next time we went to Cat Island, Burns, the handler Cobra worked with, was the lead guy. He towered over me at six foot six, with short red-brown hair and sleepy eyes. He had an anchor tattooed on his arm. Cobra said the guy was always talking about battleships and how he wished he'd joined the navy, where you ate like kings.

Burns was a good handler, though. He knew dogs.

We followed him into the jungle, six handlers, six dogs, three baits—me, Cobra, and PeeWee.

Burns brought along an attack suit, a great bulky thing he carried on his back. I would have laughed at the thought of PeeWee getting into it, because he wasn't even five feet tall. He'd get lost in there. But it wasn't funny, because if those dogs knocked him over they'd eat him alive. Why did Burns choose PeeWee for this? Maybe because PeeWee had good instincts—he knew what a dog would do even before the dog did. Still, small was small.

PeeWee whistled softly as we hiked into the jungle, the splinter scab on his cheek almost gone. Jeese, I thought, he's whistling. He has more guts than me right now.

We stopped in a big open space surrounded by trees, hazy in the heat.

"Hara," Burns said. He couldn't pronounce Cobra's last name, Uehara. "Pick one of your buddies to go first."

"I'll do it myself," Cobra said.

Burns rubbed his jaw, nodding. "No, I want you to pick one of *them*."

Cobra's jaw muscles rippled.

He pointed at me.

"You're up," Burns said. "You two pay attention. You'll get your chance."

Smith waited with the rest of the handlers. He wouldn't look at me. A chill spread through my body. I hated to be afraid. But fear came and went as it pleased.

I puffed out my cheeks and stepped forward.

Burns dumped the attack suit on the ground. "Let's get you into this."

I stared at the suit. All that protection only meant one thing—I would need it. This was like making me jump into an ocean of barracudas.

"Ain't got no snakes in it," Burns said. "Come on, put it on."

Slowly, I picked up the pieces. First, I put on canvas coveralls, then a pair of padded pants, a padded jacket, padded gloves, and a headpiece made of wire netting that sat all the way down on my shoulders to cover my throat. Then Burns pulled a hood up over my head.

I must have looked like a freak.

Within a minute, sweat poured out of my hair, dripping into my eyes. I could hardly move. When PeeWee puts this thing on, I thought, we'll never find him again.

"Take this," Burns said, handing me a small whip. "All right, form up," he said to the handlers.

Burns and the other handlers took their dogs and formed a circle around me, leaving about thirty feet between them. Smith stood ready with Kooch. Burns's dog, King, was a Labrador that looked like a small bear. Shig's pit bull, Spit, was there, too, though Shig had gone on to scout-dog training with Chik.

I hobbled around, checking out the dogs, now all around me. They looked gray and fuzzy through the wire mesh. Something big was coming. I was tight as a rock and drowning in sweat.

The handlers switched to the leather collars.

Every dog's ears turned toward me, the freak monster in the center of the circle.

Burns nodded to me. "Just do as I say, and stay alert."

He looked around at the handlers.

"Move in!"

37
THE ATTACK CIRCLE

All six dogs crept toward me, tugging at their leashes. I stood slightly crouched with my arms out, ready. I prayed I wouldn't have to move fast, because I'd just trip and fall, I knew I would, and that was what scared me the most, the thought of being on the ground with six dogs ripping into me.

Each handler walked his dog closer, saying, "Watch him," and the dogs, with heads low, closed the circle, their eyes fixed on one thing. Nothing mattered to them but the monster with that whip in its hand.

Me.

"Watch him, watch him."

When they got within five feet, the dogs were growling low and tugging so hard the handlers had to dig their heels into the sandy soil to hold them back.

"Use that whip, now," Burns said. "Just like you did with the burlap sack."

I crouched, legs spread to take on the impact if the dogs jumped on me.

Hesitantly, I brought the whip out, wagging it, threatening one dog, then another, turning around the circle, slapping at them. The dogs growled and raised their lips. Showed their fangs.

"Watch him!"

The sound of angry dogs closing in was so awful that my fear burst inside me. *"Pop!"* I called. *"Pop!"*

The dogs started lunging on every side.

I whipped at them, thinking about the ones at my back, spinning around, turning, turning, watching them all and cringing at the thought of getting blindsided.

King lunged, leaping for my face.

"Out!" Burns yelled.

King stood down, his eyes fierce.

The other handlers pulled back.

My heart slammed as I gasped for air, shaking, my legs quivering, screaming to get out of that suit and that circle right now, right now. For a moment I thought I'd peed my pants. But no, no, I hadn't.

The handlers re-formed the circle, their dogs settling beside them.

I waited, gasping.

"Stay alert," Burns said. "We're coming in again, only this time it will be one at a time . . . with no leash. They'll be snapping at you, so watch them closely. What we're doing

179

is teaching the less aggressive dogs to be more fearless, and more vicious.

"The dog will approach you in the same way, but this time when you threaten him, he will be allowed to attack you. When he does, you catch him with the sleeve on your forearm. Is that clear? Let him bite into it."

Jeese!

I tried to slow the trembling.

Stop. Think. Watch.

Kooch was first.

Smith walked him forward.

I wagged the whip.

Smith wrapped the leash around his fist.

Kooch lunged.

Smith yanked him back and got down on his knees, pulling Kooch close, whispering to him. But the dog eyed only me, just the monster, the freak, the enemy.

When Smith removed the leash, Kooch set his head low and crept in, stalking.

Silent now, way scarier than when he growled.

I stepped back.

In a blink, Kooch attacked.

I raised the sleeve as he leaped, holding my left forearm out in front of me. Kooch clamped down on it. His weight almost pulled me to the ground.

I could hear the other dogs going crazy, could even see some of them lunging at their leashes, wanting in on the action.

Kooch jerked and pulled. He tossed his head, trying to rip the sleeve off. I felt like a rag in his teeth. I stumbled forward and back, almost falling. Only my sea legs kept me on my feet.

"Out!" Smith commanded.

Instantly Kooch let go and stood down.

I staggered, breathing like a freight train, watching Burns, waiting for what would come next.

One by one, each dog came at me and took a bite out of that sleeve. One dog missed and caught me on my leg, his teeth breaking through the padding into my flesh. I buckled and fell, slapping down on him with the hard end of the whip.

The handler got him off quickly. I kicked away, scurrying back in the sand.

"Enough," Burns finally said.

When I got out of the suit I must have looked as if I'd just come out of the ocean. A haze of whiteness clouded my eyes. I felt like I was going to pass out. I hobbled back over to PeeWee and Cobra, blood swelling on my torn pant leg.

Burns tossed me a canteen. "Drink the whole thing. We'll doctor up that leg when we get back."

I caught my breath, then tipped my head back and drank until there wasn't a drop left.

Cobra's turn in that suit was coming. PeeWee's, too. But not today. Burns was done.

Cobra and PeeWee helped me limp back to the boat. The cuts were deeper than Burns cared to admit, but they didn't need stitches. Hydrogen peroxide and bandages were all I got.

"Didn't go too good today, huh?" Leroy said, pulling me aboard.

"You don't know the half of it," PeeWee said. "He's lucky to be here at all."

Leroy shook his head. "Sounds crazy."

For sure.

"Going get worse," Cobra said.

"How can it get worse?" I said. "Unless they turn all those dogs loose on us at one time."

PeeWee cringed.

Cobra fell silent, brooding the whole way back to Ship Island, carving dirt out from under his fingernails with a pocketknife.

38
THE PIG

After evening chow Chik sat on his bunk with his elbows on his knees glaring over at Golden Boy, who was censoring his latest love letter. Every now and then Golden Boy would laugh, and Chik would squirm and slug his hand with his fist.

"He laugh one more time, I going over there and re-arrange his face," Chik mumbled.

"Who's that letter to, Chik?" I asked. "Helen or Fumi?"

Chik turned and glared at me. "What you think is the meaning of the word *private*? Because that's what a letter is, ah? He shouldn't even be touching it, let alone laughing at it."

"Yeah, but it must be funny," I said. "Who you wrote it to?"

"Your ma. I told her you never stuck your nose where it don't belong. That's why Golden Boy laughing."

"Must be Fumi," I said. "Helen, you don't care that much. But Fumi—ooo la-la."

Chik jumped up and got me in a headlock, and we wrestled around until he accidentally let out a fut and we started laughing. That felt so good, to laugh.

"I like read um when you done, ah?" Shig called to Golden Boy.

Chik threw his pillow at Shig, who ducked and came up making a kissy face at Chickaboom.

Poor Chik. He was such an easy target, because he would never get mad. He just liked us to think he would.

Cobra was still quiet. Thinking about getting into that attack suit was bothering him. I knew he didn't want to do it. Who did?

I peeled off the bandages on my shin and checked out the bites. Five deep cuts shaped like dog teeth. Ricky Kondo brought over the first-aid kit and painted them with iodine, then wrapped the wounds back up with clean gauze. "Does it hurt?" he asked.

"Naah. Like a bee sting, is all."

He nodded. "That leg'll be little bit stiff in the morning, but we got the day off, so you can take it easy."

"Sounds good to me."

Golden Boy came over with Chik's letter after he'd cut out the stuff Chik wasn't supposed to say. The letter looked like a chain of cut-out dolls.

"You gave away too much classified information, lover boy. But I left all the good parts in it, all the smooching."

Chik snatched the skeleton of his letter.

"That was the closest your ugly face ever going get to girls as nice as mines, laughing boy."

❖ ❖ ❖

The next day Shig said, "Who like come look around with me? Last time I was on top the fort I saw a pig, a wild one."

"Shig," I said. "Ain't no pigs here."

"Got. I saw it."

"But pigs don't eat sand."

"Got, I tell you."

I could see he wasn't lying. Maybe it wasn't a pig, but he'd seen something. "Count me in," I said. "I got to move this leg, anyway, work out the soreness."

"Let's go."

We fought our way through scraggy low bushes and sea grass until we found pig tracks.

I studied them. "Ho, you might be right, Shig."

"Of course I'm right. They must live way down there in those trees. I wonder how pigs got on this island."

"Brought um from the mainland when they built the fort, prob'ly."

"Maybe had pigs with yellow fever and they put um here."

"Pfff."

We followed the tracks. One set. One pig.

Sometime later Shig spotted a black dot in the distance, heading away toward the trees. "There he is, look. Ho, if we can catch um, what a feast we could have."

We jogged ahead, trying to close the gap.

In the distance two small planes were heading our way from the Mississippi coast, fighters, like the Japanese ones that attacked Pearl Harbor.

I shaded my eyes. "Must be an airfield over there."

"Forget that, we got a pig to catch."

We kept following the tracks.

And the planes flew closer.

"There he is," Shig whispered, about a hundred yards away from the pig.

Minutes later the two fighters flew in over the island, angling down, making a shattering racket.

The pig started streaking in and out of the bushes.

"Hey," Shig said. "Now how we going catch it?"

The planes dropped lower.

Me and Shig froze, because they were heading straight at us. They started shooting.

Babababababababa.

Bababababababa.

The pig swerved and darted one way, then back the other way. "They shooting at that pig!" Shig said.

"Hide!" I yelled.

We dove under some shrubs and dug into the sand.

The planes kept coming, still shooting, the bullets zipping by the pig, then by us, way too close, sand erupting less than twenty yards away.

I covered my head.

Then the planes rose straight up, circled around, and headed back toward the mainland. We stood and brushed the sand off as they shrank away.

186

"Those buggas was shooting at *us*!" Shig said.

"No, they never even saw us. They were target practicing on the pig, is all."

"Could fool me."

"We ain't going catch it now," I said.

When we got back to the barracks we had the best story yet to tell the guys, only when Shig told it, there were five planes and they were shooting directly at us and we dodged bullets like football players. Some guys had even seen the planes, but they swore they had only seen two, and no one believed they fired their guns.

But who cared if they believed us or not? Everybody knew we had been getting shot at ever since Schofield—shot at with stupid work details, ugly words, marches to nowhere, angry dogs.

Nothing new.

39
HIDE TO LIVE

"You can only teach the dog one thing at a time," Smith said. "He can't concentrate on more than that."

"Pfff," I said. "Sound like some guys I know."

Smith looked at me, startled. Then he smiled. "Me too, now that I think of it."

We both chuckled.

A week had gone by, and my leg was almost healed. Cobra and PeeWee had both taken a turn inside the attack suit and survived.

Today it was just me, Smith, and Kooch.

"I heard we're sending hundreds of thousands of troops over to England," Smith said. "There's going to be a massive attack on Europe."

That news jolted me into remembering there was a war going on. "That's where we were supposed to go," I said, which was a lie. The army was never going to send us anywhere to fight.

"Then you're lucky you're here. Those guys are walking straight into a nightmare."

"We doing good in the Pacific?" I asked. "You know about that?"

"Some good, some bad, I think. Don't really know. But did you hear the Japs bombed Alaska?"

"Alaska?"

"Dutch Harbor."

"Man."

We sat thinking. What a mess this war was, a big dangerous mess, and I couldn't even fight in it.

"All right," Smith said, "we got work to do."

He put a hand on Kooch's head. "Okay. The dog knows how to track you. He knows you're the enemy, and he will attack you even when you don't have a whip or a burlap sack. He will go after you when I say so and he'll stop on command. That's all good. But we're not there yet. We got to step it up."

He ran his hand over Kooch's head, petting him, but Smith kept his eyes on me. Behind him on the ground a pair of heavy coveralls and a set of attack sleeves lay bundled on the sand.

I waited, thinking, Whatever.

I was scared, sure, because now I had a pretty good taste of how dangerous those dogs could be. But what could I do about it? Nothing. Can't be helped.

Ho, why did I think *that*?

I'm becoming Pop, I thought. Was that good or bad?

"I'm not sure you can handle this," Smith said. "I'm wondering if you have the guts."

"Anytime," I said.

The corner of Smith's mouth twitched up, just a whisper. "What was that?"

"Nothing."

Smith studied me, almost smirking. Then he took off Kooch's chain and put on the leather collar. Kooch's ears shot up. His eyes froze—on me.

Spooky.

"All right, smart boy, you understand the way this works. But now what we want is for the dog to find you using nothing but your natural Jap scent. That's been the goal all along. That's the only reason you're here."

He paused, waiting for me to react.

But there was no way would I even blink. I glared at him.

Smith grinned. "Perky today, aren't we?"

I tried not to change my expression. Like Pop.

"Anyway," Smith said, "today you're going to go out there and hide in the jungle, just like back when we first started this."

Fine, I thought. I knew about alligators and snakes. I knew where to hide. I also knew Kooch would find me no matter what I did. So how were we stepping it up?

Smith had a gleam in his eye. He winked. "Only here's the difference, Kubo: this time . . . he's going to be loose."

Something broke in my gut, like when you're on a boat and you get the first signs that you're about to throw up. "You mean no leash?" I squeaked.

"Well, I'll have him on the leash until I see that he's located you. But when that happens I'll set him free. I'll be right behind him, of course, to call him off after he attacks you, and he will. You're a Jap. We *want* him to attack you. We want him to kill, too—not you, of course, just your kind. But the dog's obedience will prevent that in this case, because when I call him off, he'll obey."

If I looked at Smith one more second I would go after him. I could feel it rising inside me. If I was Cobra, Smith would be spitting teeth.

I turned to Kooch, looked into his icy eyes with ice in my own. He didn't twitch. Kooch was somewhere else. This dog here wasn't the one who'd eaten horsemeat off my neck and kissed me back in the before time. This one had blood on his mind.

I blinked.

Smith kicked the sleeves and coveralls toward me. "The full attack suit is too bulky for what we're doing now, but these will protect you if you don't do something stupid, like turn and run."

Behind me the jungle waited. Already I was thinking about which way I'd go. Had to be good, because this dog would hunt me down no matter where I went. He would win.

But Kooch used to like me, I thought, hoping it might be true. I glanced again into those unmoving eyes, cringing when I remembered how vicious he'd been in the attack circle, the hammer of his jaws on my arm, the depth of his growl. I tried to put a smile in my eyes. You going remember I was your friend, right, boy?

Smith dipped his head toward the sleeves and coveralls. I picked them up but didn't put them on. Do that later. Now, they'd only slow me down.

"How much time I got?" I said.

"Thirty minutes. Get out there as far as you can. This is for real, now. No leash, remember."

"Who can forget?"

"I want you very hidden, you hear? I don't want him to find you by sight. I want him to smell you. When we send him to the Pacific, I want to know he's going to do his job."

"He going find me okay," I said. "Because he's prob'ly the best dog you got on this island. But it ain't going be Jap blood he smells, no. What he going smell is just me, just my scent. Human scent. Because we don't smell no diff'rent from you or anyone else."

Smith humphed. "We'll see about that soon enough, Kubo. We have a little test coming up."

"This program ain't going work," I mumbled.

"What?"

"Nothing."

"No, you said something. What was it?"

I tried to keep glaring at him but had to turn away when his eyes said, Go on, get sassy one more time and you'll see what your superiors have to say about that.

"I said *fine*."

Smith smirked. "One more thing—watch for the dog. When you see it's obvious that he's located you, I want you to reveal yourself—looking mean. I will then command you to halt and raise your hands over your head—but you will ignore me and keep up the menace. Can you do that?"

"Sure. You want me to act like I'm trying to challenge you, or kill you."

"Exactly. And the dog's going to pick up on it. You're going to trigger something deadly in him."

From the corner of my eye I could already see something deadly watching every move I made. I was the fuse; he was the bomb.

"After a short struggle, stop resisting. He'll keep ripping at the sleeve until I call him off. You will be subdued. The dog will have won. Are we clear?"

"Clear."

I ran into the jungle.

"Thirty minutes," Smith called after me. "Remember, hide like your life depends on it!"

40
JAWS
OF DEATH

The coveralls and sleeves flopped under my arm as I ran.

I came to a low spot where the grasses grew tall. There was a hidden pond that I couldn't see until I broke through the bushes and my feet were sloshing through the muck at the edges. I stopped and stepped back. I needed a stick.

I found a fallen branch and broke off part of it. Out in the water, two lumps looked back at me. Alligator eyes. But it was the snakes I worried about, because they could be anywhere. I slapped at the weeds around the water, cringing just thinking about stepping on a water moccasin. *Snick!* One bite, you could die, way out here.

There were no snakes.

But there was that alligator.

So I kept running, slapping away tree branches and spiky-leafed palmettos, racing down the skinny length of the

194

island. When I found shallow water I ran into it to try to hide my trail. I even stopped to tie palmetto leaves to my boots, making like duck feet, hoping that, too, might hide my scent. But they fell off after a couple of minutes.

I came up onto a stand of tall grass at the edge of another pond, this one larger than the last. It seemed like a good place to hide. Deep enough. Water to wash away my scent. No eyes floating like lumps.

This is the place.

But what I did wasn't smart.

First, I struggled into the coveralls and pulled on the attack sleeves; then, with my stick, I waded into the waist-high scummy brown pond.

I poked around in the marsh grass.

Boof!

A dark water moccasin shot out of the weeds and curled across the water into a bank of grass beyond. *Haaa!* My guts churned.

When my heart slowed, I took a deep breath and worked my way deeper into the grass where the snake had come from, whacking everything in front of me.

This is insane.

Using the stick, I turned back and lifted the grass I'd trampled, so I wouldn't leave a visible trail leading to my hiding place. When I got into the middle of the island of grass, I flattened down into the shallow water on my stomach and brushed the grass aside so I could see back to where Kooch would come from. Every part of me but the top of my head was submerged in the muck of brown water.

Flea-sized black bugs trailed up the reeds inches from

my face. The smell was like the swampy stink that came out of our sink on Ship Island. Mosquitoes on the surface scattered as murky warm water oozed into my coveralls and soaked my clothes.

I waited, swallowed by a ferocious silence.

Gave me the willies.

For the first time I thought about what I'd done—placed myself in a bad situation. When Kooch found me I wouldn't have any solid ground to dig my feet into. But worse than that, the padding was already soaking up water like a sponge. It would bog me down. I'd be at the mercy of chance. That just wasn't good enough.

But it was too late. No time.

I peeked through the grass, considering maybe, just maybe, Kooch wouldn't be able to follow my scent into the water and walk on by.

Not a chance.

Never in my life had I been as alert to what was around me. Everything registered. If something was there, I would notice it—bugs, snakes, scorpions, alligators, man, or dog.

I cringed at the thought of getting more dog bites. Unless Smith was fast, Kooch would tear through the soggy padding quickly and easily. And Smith hadn't given me a neck guard. I was as exposed as a chicken on a chopping block.

I swallowed dirty water while thinking that thought and choked on it, spitting the stinky bits of bugs and mud out while trying to stay quiet.

Something moved in the trees.

I held my breath, sank down.

A slinking shadow.

Then Smith.

Kooch stopped and raised his head, his ears cocked forward.

Smith came up behind him, glancing into the bushes, the trees, the buggy swamp—looking everywhere I wasn't. But he knew Kooch was on to me.

Smith squatted and took off the leash. Why I even hoped that dog might not find my scent was beyond me.

Kooch loped ahead, sniffing the ground exactly where I'd walked. Smith jogged after him.

My scalp prickled. The water went cold as my fear spread. Bad idea, hiding here. Bad, bad, bad.

Kooch knew I was close.

He followed his nose, sweeping over the sand, faster, faster, Smith plunging after him, shoving branches away, jumping over dead trees.

Kooch stopped suddenly, a low growl rumbling in his throat.

"Watch him," Smith whispered. "Find the enemy."

Kooch grew more agitated, going one way, then another, then coming back, finding the scent, losing it, closing in, and in, and in.

My heart was pounding so hard I thought Kooch might hear it.

"Good boy, watch him, now."

Kooch suddenly inhaled the scent.

So close now.

He knew.

When he was almost on me, I whooshed up out of the grass, dripping with muddy water—a monster. "Ahhh!"

Kooch jumped back. He raised his lips and snarled, a terrifying sound, something deep, dark, and ancient.

I staggered toward dry land, trying to get out of the mud, the weight of the padding doubled.

I needed solid ground. Fast.

Kooch ran parallel to me, a thin wall of grass and water separating us.

"Halt!" Smith yelled. "Put your hands over your head!"

But I kept going, like Smith had told me to do, now almost out of the water.

"Get him! Kill!"

Kooch sprang ahead, charging.

Before I slogged free of the weeds, I turned and braced for the impact, because I knew he was going to hit like a truck. His iron jaws would rip me to pieces if I didn't do this right.

He leaped, up and up.

Flying.

I raised my left arm as he came down on me. His jaws clamped on the padded sleeve. I staggered under the weight, like a hundred-pound bag of sand tumbling down on me.

Down, down.

Falling back.

I hit water. Went under.

Kooch was attached to my arm, yanking me one way and the next.

I came up for air, pushing back, his jaws still clamped on

the sleeve. I tried to roll away, to get out from under him. But he had the power, all of it.

I yelped when he ripped the sleeve off my arm.

For a second Kooch was confused. Sleeve in his jaws, with no man. He dropped it.

I backed away on my hands, still sitting in the mud.

Mind blank.

Staring into bloodthirsty ice-pick eyes.

In a blink, Kooch lunged for my throat, just like he remembered from before, like he was trained to do—where the reward was, the meat, the wet blood.

I fell back and tried to lift the other sleeve.

Too late.

He pushed past the sleeve. His breath fell on me, hot.

I'm dead, I'm dead.

"Kooch," I gasped, gagging on my fear. "No—"

I was about to die.

But what I saw in my head in that moment was him coming up to kiss me, to lick my face like he did in the first days. Kissing, kissing. Good dog, Kooch, my friend, good friendly dog. Somebody's pet.

His teeth scraped my jaw, trying to get to my neck. I could feel the sharp points. I squeezed my eyes shut. *"Smith!"* I yelled. "Get him off!"

Smith was a blur running toward me, a look of horror on his face, his mouth gaped open.

Saying nothing.

Not Out.

Not Stop.

I raised my naked arm to protect my neck. Kooch bit down. *"Ahhhhh!"*

"Out!" Smith finally yelled. "Out!"

Kooch let go, backed off, growling, a deep and terrifying sound. He stood waiting for Smith with his hackles up, waiting for the command: Kill! Kill! Kill!

I leaped up, blood oozing from my arm. *"Why didn't you call him off soon as he hit me!"*

I charged.

Smith was off balance when I plowed into him. He went down, and I pounded him with the clubs of my fists.

Kooch charged in, snarling and tearing at both of us.

But I kept fighting.

"Stop, stop!" Smith shouted, pushing me back.

But it was Kooch, not Smith, who brought me back to my senses. The dog would kill us both if we didn't do something fast. I stopped.

"Out!" Smith shouted. "Out!"

Kooch, confused, lips high and wild and teeth like yellow death, backed off, the rumbling in his throat like distant thunder.

Smith, gasping, leaped up and collared him. Through his ripped shirt I could see the bloody cuts on his chest where Kooch had ripped into him. Smith's hands shook. His face was ghost white and beaded with sweat and muddy water. When he saw me looking at him, his eyes dropped.

We sat back in the dirt, catching our breath. Kooch stood with his legs spread, head low, watching us.

Then, slowly, he lay down.

Panting. Resting.

✢ ✢ ✢

We headed back through the jungle in silence, Smith and Kooch a step ahead of me, when they should have been behind me, as if keeping a close watch over their prisoner.

I staggered to keep my balance when a wave of sudden dizziness clouded my vision. Delayed reaction. I felt like throwing up.

Smith and Kooch picked up the pace, now almost out of sight ahead of me.

I took a step, and another.

Moving on, blood badges staining my shirt.

41
MR. PURPLE
HEART

That night on Ship Island I climbed to the top of Fort Massachusetts in the dark and lay flat on my back looking up at the stars. My cuts were not as bad as Smith's, who probably had to get a few stitches. Still, my wounds stung under the new bandages.

It smelled fishy up there.

A good smell that made me feel alive, and safe.

Peaceful.

The stars twinkled bright as campfires.

Funny, but those stars seemed different to me now. For probably the first time in my life I saw them and actually thought about them. When you almost die you pay more attention. I thought about my life and my friends, and how we were all in this war together, bleeding the same blood, taking what was dished out by those above us, following

orders—me and my Cat Island brothers, who all sympa-
thized over my new dog bites, calling me Mr. Purple Heart.

It was just what I needed.

As I lay there, the air cooled, slow and easy. I calmed
down, not as much as I wanted to, but enough. What about
Smith? Was he shook up, too?

Yes.

Who wouldn't be?

A while later, I went back to my bunk and kept to myself, me and my good-luck stone. I had to remember to
thank Herbie for that, because on this day luck had let me
live.

The rest of the guys lounged around talking low until
Ricky Kondo decided to bring out a small stack of letters that
had come in with Leroy.

"Eddy," he said. "Looks like somebody loves you after
all."

It was from Herbie.

But I was still too shaky to open it.

"We got three days off," Ricky said, waving an official-
looking letter. "Brass coming after that."

"What brass?" PeeWee said.

"The major and some big shots from Washington coming
to see how the K-9 program is working."

"It's working," Chik said. "Those dogs are dangerous.
Look at Eddy."

"That was their goal," Ricky said. "Smell us, hate us, attack us on sight. Remember Parrish said that?"

Nods and mumbles rolled around the room.

"Eddy, you did the best at making your dog hate you,"

PeeWee said. "That's what they coming to see, ah? You just show them those scars."

More nods. "Yeah, Eddy, ain't nobody better than you."

I remembered something Smith had said about a little test. Was this it? Some show for the guys making the big decisions?

PeeWee and Golden Boy got a game of cards going. Cobra went to sleep. Outside, Ricky Kondo sat by himself in the dark.

I settled on the floor with my back against my bunk and tore open Herbie's letter, the only one I'd ever gotten from him. But that was okay. He had enough to worry about.

> *Eddy.*
>
> *Pop finished the sampan today, the one he was making for the haole in Kaneohe to replace the one that burned up. Lucky the new owner is a white guy, because Pop can't make boats for Japanese now. The boat looks good. He won't take it out for a test until he got the haole on board. If it works, he just going give the guy the boat right then.*
>
> *Still now nobody knows why the first one blew up. Pop says it's not important to know why, and to forget it. It would only bring more trouble to know. What happened, happened. That's what he said. But I don't think he thinks it was an accident. Me either. What I think is somebody blew it up on purpose. But who can prove it? And what you going do even if you can?*

Nothing. Only make it worse. So maybe Pop is right. But how can you just walk away, Eddy? Makes me too mad. You know what they did to my friend's boat? You remember the Taiyo Maru, *Nakaji's boat? The FBI or the army or somebody took it up the canal past the rice fields and put a hole in it. Sank it, Eddy! Just because it was a Japanese boat. And that ain't right. His boy, Tomi, going try bring it up.*

Well, other than that, I'm good and so is Ma. She volunteers at the Red Cross one day a week, making socks. Get this, she says it makes her feel like she's fighting the war right alongside you. Crazy, yeah?

Are you anywhere near the fighting? I hope not. What I see in the papers is terrible. Bodies of dead guys, blown-up towns. Have you heard of an island called Guadalcanal? It's in the South Pacific. Well, there was a big fight there between us and Japan. Lasted about six months. We won it, but lot of guys died, Eddy. On both sides. I hope you aren't anywhere like that.

Well, this is too long, so I'll sign off now.

Oh yeah, one more thing. Ugly Sharky and Opah both just dragging around. Pop says it's because of you were too nice to them before. Now they can't live without you. They lovesick.

Bye.

Herbie Okubo.

I chuckled and folded the letter back into the envelope. Funny how he signed it Herbie Okubo, like he thought maybe I didn't remember his last name.

I shook my head.

You wrong, Pop.

You got to fight back. You don't, you lose your self-respect.

But what about when they don't *let* you fight?

I got up off the floor and plopped down on my bunk. When I closed my eyes I heard Pop's voice.

Ganbare, Eddy. *Ganbare.*

Keep going.

I rolled over and covered my head with my pillow.

42
THE CITY SHOES

Four days later, Leroy eased the *Sugar Babe* in toward the island, one hand on the wheel, the other raised in salute. Me, Cobra, and Ricky Kondo were sitting on the pier, fishing.

Leroy smiled up at us, the idling boat rumbling easy on the water. "Ah-low-*ha*," he said with a grin. "That how y'all say it back t'home?"

"Only if you one haole," Cobra said.

"One what?"

"Don't worry. You pass."

"We working today?" Ricky asked.

"Yup. Just dropped some men in suits off over to Cat. They're waiting on y'all."

"They like the cow rays?" I said.

Leroy snorted. "You kidding? I let them city shoes off on the other side at the pier."

"Oh. Forgot about that."

Leroy tossed up a line. "Apparently they're here to see how y'alls are working out."

"They say who they were?"

"Nope, but they looked important."

Ricky frowned. Again, he'd been skipped when the information was handed out. "Well, I guess we better go find out what's going on, then," he said.

"Your major just asked for . . . Wait a minute."

Leroy pulled a scrap of paper from his pocket. Stumbling through the pronunciation, he read, "Okubo, Uehara, Okazaki, Matsumaru, and Kondo."

"Major Parrish?" I said. "He's over there?"

"Uh-huh."

A half hour later we boarded the *Sugar Babe*. Everybody else got to stay behind and go fishing.

"No worry," Slim called from the pier. "We save you some sea trout, ah."

"You do that," Cobra said as the boat pulled away, "because the *real* men going come back *real* hungry, ah? Make us a nice meal, now."

Slim grinned.

Boy, was I going to miss all this when it was over. Strange, I know, but this island was like a home to me now.

Chik started singing.

"You're in the army now, you're not behind a plow, you'll never get rich by digging a ditch, you're in the army now."

Pretty soon all of us were hooting and swaying, singing it over and over, like that other song that gives you a headache, "Ninety-nine Bottles of Beer on the Wall."

❖ ❖ ❖

At Cat Island, we waded ashore and hiked through the trees to our meeting spot. My stomach was rising, making me feel sick. I wasn't scared; I just wasn't ready.

Seven men were waiting for us.

Four strangers I took for Leroy's city-shoes guys—and Major Parrish, the Swiss. And Sweet.

What was *he* doing here?

We stood in a half circle facing them. The attack dogs and their handlers were grouped up by the kennels under a clear blue sky. Smith was there in front, looking down, his hand on Kooch's head. One of his arms was bandaged, but otherwise he looked like always. I wondered how he'd explained those bites.

"Good morning, men," Major Parrish said. "You know Franz, of course, and Lieutenant Sweet."

Sweet winked.

Major Parrish swung his hand toward the city shoes. "These men came down from Washington, D.C., to see how your part in the war dog program is progressing."

The men dipped their heads, nodded. Seemed like okay guys.

"Earlier this year, Franz convinced President Roosevelt that he could train dogs to identify Japanese soldiers by their scent. That's what these men from Washington are here to see."

I glanced at Smith, but he wouldn't look at me.

"They want a scent, we should go get Leroy," Chik whispered.

Cobra smirked.

The Swiss nodded to the guys from Washington, then motioned for Smith and Kooch to step forward.

"You," he said, pointing to me. "Front and center."

I glanced at Chik and Cobra, then stepped up.

Smith stood waiting with Kooch, who sat obediently to his left. This time when I looked at Smith, he looked back.

I held his gaze.

He dipped his chin, slightly.

The Swiss then called on three guys from the Quartermaster Corps, not handlers. Guys I'd never seen before.

I leaned close and whispered to Smith, "You get cut bad?"

"Naw. The gator got it worse."

I had to smile.

"All right," the Swiss said to the city shoes. "I'm sending four men out to hide. Note that their only difference is their race—three Americans, and one Jap."

Jeese! I thought. What's *wrong* with these idiots? I glanced at Smith, now standing with his lips pursed, looking at his feet.

"The dog will have four scents to follow. He will choose the Jap scent, because that's what he's been trained to do. That will be proof of his particular ability."

The Swiss put a hand on my shoulder. "When the dog finds you, stand up and put your hands in the air. You know what to do."

I nodded.

Kooch's ears cocked forward.

210

How was this a test? Kooch always found me. The Swiss should have picked somebody Kooch didn't know. Because if Kooch sniffed out one of the white guys when he knew me so well, then this program was in big trouble. Strange, but that thought made me sad, because of all the work we'd put into this.

"Head off into the woods and hide, all of you," the Swiss said. "Not too far, now. We want to see the dog perform."

The Swiss had Smith distract Kooch so he wouldn't see where we went.

We spread out.

I found a place just inside the jungle, a sandy hole under a leafy green bush. By now Kooch had taught me a thing or two about hiding; how to toss sand over my footprints to try to mask the scent; how to sit as still as a lizard, barely breathing, blending into the shadows, making no sound. Becoming the landscape. Invisible.

Unblinking, I peeked through the leaves.

And waited.

A cold river shuddered through me. I wanted to throw up, remembering the last time Kooch had come looking for me. I inched my hand toward my pocket for the blue stone. It wasn't there. Did I lose it?

"All right," the Swiss called.

Smith took the chain off Kooch and replaced it with the leather collar. He used the six-foot leash. Man and dog moved toward the trees.

"Watch him," Smith said.

Kooch sniffed the ground, back and forth, picking up the scents. Mine he knew as well as Smith's, and I cringed, thinking that it was right up front in his memory because of the bloody fight the last time we met.

The Swiss watched with his hands on his hips.

I didn't move a muscle, keeping as still as I possibly could, sweat dripping off me like rain. If Kooch came to me it would just be because he knew me. That was all. He knew me as well as he knew Smith or the family that had volunteered him for the army.

"Watch him," Smith said again.

It can't work. How could I face Smith's smirk if it did? Or ever in my life tell Pop about this? Or anyone? How could I say we had some kind of special stink dogs can pick up on? Impossible.

Kooch stopped, his ears pricked ahead. He tugged on the leash, and Smith let the dog lead him.

I was soaked in sweat, the memory of the fight with Smith and Kooch pouring back into me.

Closer, closer.

Coming in.

Kooch stopped and grumbled, low and frightening. I squeezed my eyes shut.

I heard a rustle in the bushes and covered my head with my arms. Kooch growled louder.

Somebody yelped.

"Out!" Smith called.

I snapped up.

It wasn't me Kooch had found.

One of the white guys stood with his hands in the air, his face white.

Kooch stood with his eyes fixed on the guy.

I took a deep breath, almost gasping. Was it true?

Something broke and flooded out of me. I could feel it. I sank down into the dirt.

It's over.

Over.

But it didn't make me feel any better, because right or wrong, something I'd given so much for had just failed.

All of us hiding in the bushes moved out into the silence. The Swiss, standing back with the Washington big shots, didn't seem to know what to do next.

Smith got down on one knee and praised Kooch for finding his man. Then he peeked up at me.

He glanced back to be sure no one else could hear, then said, "Just so you know, Kubo . . . I never . . . I never did buy into that Jap smell thing."

I scowled. "How come you didn't say that before now?"

"Why should I? Japs ain't nobody's favorite people these days, you know."

I looked down. Then back up.

Smith, gazing at Kooch now, said, "I pegged you wrong, Kubo. Sorry. "

He stood and brushed the sand from his knee.

I watched him walk Kooch back toward the other handlers, not knowing what to do with what I'd just heard.

I guess I should have felt some sense of triumph. But all I felt was worn out. We were just soldiers, doing our jobs. Me and Smith and Kooch.

The Swiss stood for long minutes with his hands frozen on his hips.

                            ✢ ✢ ✢

   On the boat heading back to Ship Island we all knew that
our time here was over. If the dogs couldn't find us just because we were Japanese, then what was the use of Japanese
dog bait?

   I don't know why, but right then I thought of President
Roosevelt and how he believed we might smell different
from white guys.

   My president.

   Made me feel sad.

43
SHADOW
OF WAR

A day later I was fishing off the pier with a bamboo pole and fiddler crab bait. Some of the guys were back at the barrack. Others had gone swimming on the other side of the island or hiking down the coast, enjoying the last days of our wartime paradise, because when the city shoes left, they looked grim.

Chik and Cobra sat next to me, the three of us talking about old times back home in Kaka'ako.

"Remember that goofy guy from Coral Street?" Chik said. "What was his name? The guy always skipping school?"

"Harvey," Cobra said.

"Yeah, Harvey. Remember when he said his teacher was making his class read a book called *Homeless Idiot?*"

We all laughed, remembering. It felt good to think back on something so clear, now that our future was so foggy.

"Was Homer's *Iliad,* ah?" Chik shook his head. "He should be in the army. Make him a lieutenant, like Sweet."

I snorted.

But I couldn't shake the memory of the grim faces on those city shoes, standing around so quiet after Kooch went to the white guy. That moment changed the path of our lives.

I shook my head and looked up, then raised my hand to block the sun. "Look . . . Leroy coming."

The *Sugar Babe* was heading over from Cat Island with some guy standing on the bow. "Only one guy I know stands like that," I said.

Chik and Cobra leaned forward to look past me.

"How come he shows up everywhere we go?"

"He must love you," Cobra said.

"He love to make me do push-ups, you mean."

"That, too."

"Look who else is on board," Chik said.

Major Parrish was just ducking up the companionway, coming out on deck. "Prob'ly checking out Leroy's new fuel pump, make sure the army got its money's worth."

"Hunh," Cobra grunted.

Leroy aimed the boat toward the pier.

We stood and hauled up our lines. Four fat sea trout were curved into a bucket of seawater next to us.

Leroy reversed the engines just as the *Sugar Babe* was about to ram the pier.

Sweet tossed up the coiled bow line. Major Parrish hopped off and secured the stern. "Afternoon, men," he said. "Good fishing?"

"Yes, sir," we said, saluting him.

He gave a casual salute back. "You rested up?"

"Feeling fine, sir," Chik said.

"Good, because we've got new orders."

✛ ✛ ✛

That evening Hot Dog made up a special dinner from all the fish everyone caught, like a party at home in Japanese camp. Even Sweet had a good time.

"Gather round, men," Major Parrish said finally.

We found places to sit on the floor and bunks, ready for the bad news. It was always bad. I figured we'd be sent back to McCoy, where they'd tell us we weren't fit to fight.

Major Parrish paced with his hands in his pockets. "Let's start with the obvious—your mission here has been terminated. Washington wasn't impressed. Nevertheless, your work was excellent. A very difficult job."

Sweet stood off to the side, cleaning his ear with his little finger.

Major Parrish looked at the floor. "I wasn't so sure about that Japanese scent business. But the president bought it, and that's all that mattered."

"They should have fed us that smelly stuff they eat in Japan," Ricky Kondo said. "*Koko, natto,* and *takuwan*—that would have done it."

We all laughed, because if that didn't do it, nothing would.

"Maybe so, maybe so," Major Parrish said. "But I commend you all, because you were entirely successful in all other areas of the work you did here—especially with the scout and sentry dogs. And those of you working with the attack dogs performed bravely and with discipline."

I winced, remembering what Smith had told me about the suicide dogs.

"A few of you will go to Gulfport to continue working with the sentry dogs. The rest of you are heading to Camp Shelby, Mississippi, to rejoin your battalion for advanced-unit training."

A groan rumbled through the room, because we all knew how out of shape we were—sleeping late, fishing, swimming, eating all that good seafood. Ho, would we pay, just to get back to where we were before. I rubbed my arm, my dog bites down to scabs now. I was ready.

"You've got seven days to pack up. Meanwhile, enjoy yourselves, because once you leave this island things are going to change drastically."

Major Parrish studied our faces, just like he used to do back in mechanical drawing class at McKinley. "This is it, boys. You're going to Europe. You're going to war."

44
AMERICANS

These islands were just sandbars on a flat gulf. From a distance, you could hardly even see them. Blips on the water. But I knew my memories of them would follow me every day of my life.

Which could be a long time.

Or not.

Because the U.S. Army was finally going to let us do our part. "I know how you've been treated," Major Parrish had told us, "and I don't blame you for having your doubts about how people feel about you. But you've proved your worth and your loyalty ten times over, as I knew you would, even in the minds of your most stalwart critics. I hope you are as proud of how you've served as I am."

A new wave of pride began to grow inside me, a swelling in my chest. The major had always believed in us. His words brought back those feelings I had when I joined up, the sense of doing something to right the wrong that had been done to us—to Pop. Later, it had grown to include all those innocent people behind the fence at Camp McCoy. Americans. People who had done no wrong.

I was a U.S. Army soldier.

I did my job.

Nobody beat me down.

✛ ✛ ✛

The mood was somber the day we loaded our equipment onto the *Sugar Babe*. It was late afternoon when we pulled away from the pier. The water was calm and silky, as if wanting to give us its best farewell.

I sat with Cobra up near Leroy at the wheel.

Behind us the islands sank slowly down into the gulf. Leroy was quiet, his hands easing the wheel to the movement of the water.

"I ain't going to forget this time in my life," he said out of the blue, kind of shy. "I gotten to know you folks . . . and . . . well, you ain't nothing but honest-to-goodness decent fellows, and I'm proud to know you."

Cobra turned and squinted at him, then grinned. "You ain't so bad yourself," he said.

"But you kind of worthless when your boat gets broke," I added.

Leroy chuckled. "Ain't that the truth."

I was going to miss Leroy, stinky clothes and all.

We sat silent.

I wondered if Kooch would miss me. Probably not—but I was sure going to miss him, even if he did tear me up. But he tore up Smith, too.

Smith.

Just a kid like me, doing his duty. He hated some of what we had to do to those dogs. It was hard for him, too.

I'd thought a long time about that look he'd given me just before the test, when he locked onto my eyes and dipped his chin. Because that was it, everything right then and there—all I ever wanted from this army, or even from this country—*everything* was in that one look.

Respect.

All the rot I had to go through before that moment was worth it, just for that one thing.

Now we were equals.

I would go into battle with my head held high.

Go for broke!

Because I was a soldier.

An American.

I glanced back at Chik. His eyes were closed, probably dreaming about Helen or Fumi. I grinned and shook my head.

Cobra tapped my arm and pointed back to the islands. "Almost gone now."

I nodded and gulped down one more deep breath of sweet salt air. "Even though it was bad, it was good," I said.

"Yeah."

"I going remember Kooch. Almost as scrappy as Sharky."

"Pfff." Cobra sighed. "Rat Dog, you mean."

I smiled.

Then I remembered where we were going. To Europe, to war, where Leroy said soldiers like me were dying by the truckload.

I looked back, one last time. The islands were gone now, swallowed by the sea.

I'd be lying if I said I wasn't afraid.

AUTHOR'S NOTE

Eyes of the Emperor is a work of fiction.

However, as is its companion novel, *Under the Blood-Red Sun*, it is based on factual events and incidents of World War II.

I have left some actual names within the story—Slim (Taneyoshi Nakano), James (James Komatsu), Ray (Raymond Nosaka), and Tokuji (Tokuji Ono). And the scene where Slim swims out to help James in the storm relates an actual incident. Slim was awarded the Soldier's Medal for his act of bravery.

Other parts of the story are factual as well.

Off Bellows Field in Waimanalo, Oahu, Japanese Naval Ensign Kazuo Sakamaki became America's first prisoner of war, captured by Sergeant David Akui of the 298th Infantry. Sakamaki was subsequently imprisoned at Camp McCoy, Wisconsin, where he is said to have disfigured his face with cigarettes as a result of his own deep shame.

At Schofield Barracks in the days following the attack on Pearl Harbor, U.S. soldiers of Japanese ancestry were isolated from the other men and woke one morning surrounded by machine guns. No explanation was ever given them.

The twenty-six Hawaiian Americans of Japanese ancestry to whom I have dedicated this novel were handpicked for

223

top-secret K-9 training on Cat Island, Mississippi. A former Swiss hunting guide had apparently convinced President Franklin D. Roosevelt that the Japanese race exuded a distinct scent that dogs could be trained to discern.

The program failed.

However, the K-9 Corps in general (then called Dogs for Defense) proved highly successful for the United States military. Between 1942 and 1945, 30 breeds and 19,000 dogs were accepted for service. Dogs have been serving valiantly ever since.

I have been profoundly fortunate in having met and interviewed eight of the twenty-six Cat Island men—Raymond Nosaka (and his gracious wife, Aki), Katsumi Maeda, Koyei Matsumoto, Toshio Mizusawa, Tokuji Ono, Billy Takaezu, Seiji Tanigawa, and Yasuo Takata. Sixty years after their Cat Island experience, their wartime camaraderie is as strong as ever. I found them all warm, welcoming, friendly, and humble.

"I was proud to do my part," Tokuji Ono said.

And Ray Nosaka had this hope: "Remember us, so that we won't be forgotten."

✤ ✤ ✤

Masao Hatanaka, James Komatsu, and Patrick Tokushima were killed in action in Italy. Slim Nakano and James Komatsu both earned Silver Stars. Yukio Yokota earned the Distinguished Service Cross. Fred Kanemura received a Field Commission. Every man who served on Cat Island received at least one Purple Heart and a Bronze Star.

❖ ❖ ❖

Today, Cat Island is much as it was in the early 1940s. Except for a few fishing structures along an interior man-made canal, the island remains pristine. It is privately owned and is not accessible, except by invitation.

Ship Island can be reached by ferry from Gulfport, Mississippi. In 1969, the two-hundred-mile-an-hour winds and thirty-foot tide of Hurricane Camille cut the island in two. The reconstructed lighthouse and old Fort Massachusetts still stand. Ship Island is protected by the National Park Service.

Through the generosity of filmmaker Barry Foster and his fishing pal, Ted Riemann, I was given a private tour of both islands.

As we walked through the trees, I saw the remains of shelters and rusted machinery of the Quartermaster camp, and I had the eerie feeling that I'd just stepped back to 1942.

❖ ❖ ❖

To the men of Cat Island, Third Platoon, Company B:
Thank you for your example.
Thank you for your heroism.
Thank you for your service.
You have honored us all.

GLOSSARY

HAWAIIAN
haole - white person, Caucasian
moi - Pacific threadfin fish

HAWAIIAN PIDGIN ENGLISH
babooze - clown
bazooks - idiots (endearing)
bolohead - baldheaded
bombye - by and by, later
ete - someone who doesn't fit in
mempachi eyes - bug-eyes

JAPANESE
bakatare - fool, crazy man
dame ohsi - making doubly sure
ganbare - hold on, keep going, persevere
haji - shame
hinomaru - the red sun, symbol of Japan
Hirohito - the 124th emperor of Japan
issei - first-generation Japanese
immigrant
koko - pickled turnip (also *okoko*); salty
pickled vegetables, chopped into small
pieces and eaten with rice
Masaka! - Never! It couldn't be!
Moshimoshi - said when answering the phone

Nandato?- What did you say? (with anger)
natto - fermented soybeans
nisei - second-generation Japanese American
Shikataganai - It can't be helped.
takuwan - pickled daikon; Japanese radish
Yamato Damashii - the spirit of Japan

For more information on the contribution and service of Americans of Japanese ancestry in World War II, please visit www.GoForBroke.org.

AMERICANISM IS A MATTER OF THE
MIND AND HEART; AMERICANISM IS NOT,
AND NEVER WAS, A MATTER
OF RACE OR ANCESTRY.

—FRANKLIN D. ROOSEVELT,
1943

GRAHAM SALISBURY'S family has lived in the Hawaiian Islands since the early 1800s. He grew up on Oahu and Hawaii and graduated from California State University. He received an MFA from Vermont College of Norwich University, where he was a member of the founding faculty of the MFA program in writing for children. He lives with his family in Portland, Oregon.

Graham Salisbury's books have garnered many prizes. *Blue Skin of the Sea* won the Bank Street Child Study Association Award and the Oregon Book Award; *Under the Blood-Red Sun* won the Scott O'Dell Award for Historical Fiction, the Oregon Book Award, Hawaii's Nene Award, and the California Young Reader Medal; *Shark Bait* won the Oregon Book Award and a *Parents' Choice* Silver Honor; *Lord of the Deep* won the *Boston Globe–Horn Book* Award for fiction. *Jungle Dogs* was an ALA Best Book for Young Adults, and Graham Salisbury's most recent book, *Island Boyz: Stories,* was a *Booklist* Editors' Choice.

Graham Salisbury has been a recipient of the John Unterecker Award for Fiction and the PEN/Norma Klein Award.

GRAHAM SALISBURY

EYES OF THE
EMPEROR

A READERS GUIDE

1. Pop is a very strong character in the book. What do you think of the way he treats Eddy? Can you understand why he ignores Eddy when Eddy tells him he has enlisted in the army?

2. Do you think Eddy is right to lie about his age so that he can serve his country?

3. Are there points in the story at which you can understand the prejudices and fear that Lieutenant Sweet and other characters feel? What do you think of the way they act toward the Japanese Americans, especially Eddy and his friends?

4. Eddy is angry when he is called a Jap, and he speaks out against the use of this word, yet he sometimes calls whites *haole*, which simply means "white" in Hawaiian. Characters in the book also refer to "locals," who are any nonwhites raised in Hawaii. These words reflect a history of race and class conflict in Hawaii, and *haole* can be used as a highly charged and demeaning epithet. How do you feel about Eddy's use of this word?

5. Before Eddy is sent to Mississippi, his troop travels to Camp McCoy, where he once again runs into Sakamaki. Sakamaki makes only two appearances in the book. Why do you think he's important to the story, and what do you think of his actions?

6. When the boys are told that their job as they are training the dogs is to be the bait, they are terrified. Why do you think no one speaks out against this decision?

7. In the end, Smith tells Eddy that he never believed that the Japanese had a different scent. What does this say about Smith? What do you think of him as a character? Do you think he changes over the course of the story, or has he always believed this and just didn't want to disobey orders?

8. Leroy is a good friend to the soldiers on Cat Island. When the *Sugar Babe* stalls and the coast guard opens fire on them, he stands by the men on his boat. Why do you think he is important to the story?

9. Reread the first and last lines of the novel. What does Eddy feel at the start and at the end? Why did the author use these lines to begin and end his story?

To read Graham Salisbury's answers
to these questions, visit his Web site:
www.grahamsalisbury.com

IN HIS
OWN WORDS

A CONVERSATION WITH
GRAHAM SALISBURY

JEFF PFEFFER

Q. What inspired you to write this story? Why did Eddy appeal to you as a protagonist?
A. I was inspired not so much by Eddy, but by the story itself. *Eyes of the Emperor* is based on real history—on something I had never heard of before, and something that whacked me upside the head when I discovered it while doing some general World War II research. That "Oh, wow!" moment of discovery was my inspiration. When Eddy jumped up and wanted to play the main role, I asked him a few questions. I liked his answers and hired him on the spot.

Q. In two of your other books, *Under the Blood-Red Sun* and *House of the Red Fish*, you've also written about Japanese Americans living in Hawaii and the prejudice they face during World War II. Why do this era and setting hold such appeal for you as a writer?
A. The story of the American of Japanese ancestry, in Hawaii and on the mainland, is a powerful one. The story of how one group, especially one so loyal to the American way of life, could be so wrongfully treated tells of some basic fear that lives in the American psyche. We are a good people. We are generous and forgiving. Yet we own some kind of deep-rooted fear that has, at times, ripped the goodness and generosity right out of our hearts. Having grown up in the islands, I know somewhat of the Japanese living there. I know that as a whole they are as good and generous and accepting as any other decent American. When I look at what our government did to them in World War II, and how they, the JAs, fought to prove their loyalty to that very same government, I am impressed. Actually, I am impressed and fascinated. Would I have had such courage? Would you?

Q. What was the most difficult part of writing this book?
A. Getting beyond the guilt of writing someone else's story, someone else's history. In fact, I would not have undertaken this project at all had the men involved wished me to stay out of it. The first thing I did upon interviewing the men I was fortunate enough to have met was to ask them if I could tell their story, because it wasn't mine. I had not lived it. Not one of them objected. Still, I tiptoed my way into this story, even though I was screaming to tell it. That was the toughest part of the entire writing process.

Q. What will happen to Eddy next?
A. He will be sent to Europe and will fight the Germans alongside Chik and Cobra. He will see and do things that will challenge his humanity and test him to the extreme.

Q. What do you like best about being a writer?
A. I love the magic that happens when I am working (the surprises that come out of nowhere), and the thrill of discovering a story that would be stunning to tell. *Eyes of the Emperor* was one of those stories. When I first discovered it (in a three-page essay written by one of the Cat Island men, Raymond Nosaka), it grabbed me and shook me and said *You have to tell this story!* Now, that's exciting stuff.

Q. Tell us about your writing habits.
A. I am a morning person. I do my best work before 10:00 a.m. I get up at 4:45 every weekday. I work best when I am away from my e-mail (which is *so* much easier than *working!*). So before I go to my studio (a 900-square-foot cabana built on a pier out over a lake), I go to any one of several favorite coffee shops and work there. I write first drafts in longhand and revise on my Mac. I like the white noise of other

6

people bustling about. I try my best to write every day except weekends, which I reserve for my family. Discipline is a key element. I am not a genius. I have to make it happen. There is no other way.

Q. Do you eat snacks while you write?
A. No. I get too deep down into my imagination to think about snacks (but I do drink one cup of coffee a day—a twelve-ounce Americano with a tad of nonfat milk stirred in). When I surface, I'm usually famished and ready to hit the gym. I eat lunch after the gym, and sometimes in the hot months get a Jamba Juice as I head back to work (Orange Dream Machine).

Q. Do you listen to music while writing?
A. Never. I may listen to very soft, very calm instrumental music while revising, but never when involved in a first draft. The one exception to this took place when I was writing the first draft of a short story called "Angel-Baby," when I listened to Houston Person's luxurious rendering of "But Beautiful" (on his CD called *My Romance*). You will see why if you read that story (it's in my short story collection *Island Boyz*).

Q. How much research do you have to do before writing a book? Where do you do it?
A. It all depends on the project. For the war books, research is key. I want my facts to be as accurate as possible. I do my best research in the same place I do my best writing—in coffee shops, except when I need to ply the Net (I don't do coffee shop hot spots, because I want to keep the Net out of that workspace). If I need to search the Internet, I go to my cabana and work there. I also have access to a research professional when the research demands an expertise I don't have. She

lives in Idaho and is wonderful. But the best kind of research I can do (if possible) is primary research, where I interview people who were actually present during whatever piece of history I am writing about. *That* is a thrill!

Q. Do you ever get writer's block?
A. I get lazy, I get stuck, I dink around—but I never get writer's block. Writer's block to me is one thing and one thing only: procrastination. I try to keep moving ahead, even if I hate what I'm producing. You see, I have learned something valuable over my years of writing: whatever drivel I produce, I can fix. I work hard. Most of the time.

Q. As a writer, what is your greatest fear? Your greatest obstacle?
A. As a writer I have few fears. However, I do have a good deal of self-doubt. Am I really good enough to continue writing stories of value for young readers? So far, I believe I am (any writer has to have that self-belief to succeed). I guess if I have a fear at all, it would be the fear of losing that confidence. Yeah, that would be it.

Q. How much rewriting and revising do you do?
A. A lot! Over and over and over until I think it sings. Then I send it to my editor and she sends it back saying, "You can do better." And she's always right. I can, and do. God bless good editors, and I have one of the best ever. Revise, revise, revise. It will shower you with sparkling diamonds every time.

The Watsons Go to Birmingham—1963
Christopher Paul Curtis
978-0-440-41412-4
Nine-year-old Kenny lives with his middle-class black family, the Weird Watsons of Flint, Michigan. When Kenny's thirteen-year-old brother, Byron, gets to be too much trouble, they head south to Birmingham to visit Grandma, the one person who can shape him up. And they happen to be in Birmingham when Grandma's church is bombed.

The Giver
Lois Lowry
978-0-440-23768-6
Jonas's world is perfect. Everything is under control. There is no war or fear or pain. There are no choices, until Jonas is given an opportunity that will change his world forever.

Before We Were Free
Julia Alvarez
978-0-440-23784-6
Under a dictatorship in the Dominican Republic in 1960, young Anita lives through a fight for freedom that changes her world forever.

Cuba 15
Nancy Osa
978-0-385-73233-8
Violet Paz's upcoming *quinceañero*, a girl's traditional fifteenth-birthday coming-of-age ceremony, awakens her interest in her Cuban roots—and sparks a fire of conflicting feelings about Cuba within her family.

Counting Stars • David Almond • 978-0-440-41826-9
With stories that shimmer and vibrate in the bright heat of memory, David Almond creates a glowing mosaic of his life growing up in a large, loving Catholic family in northeastern England.

Heaven Eyes • David Almond • 978-0-440-22910-0
Erin Law and her friends in the orphanage are labeled Damaged Children. They run away one night, traveling downriver on a raft. What they find on their journey is stranger than you can imagine.

Kit's Wilderness • David Almond • 978-0-440-41605-0
Kit Watson and John Askew look for the childhood ghosts of their long-gone ancestors in the mines of Stoneygate.

Skellig • David Almond • 978-0-440-22908-7
Michael feels helpless because of his baby sister's illness, until he meets a creature called Skellig.

Finding Miracles • Julia Alvarez • 978-0-553-49406-8
Fifteen-year old Milly has never told anyone in her small Vermont town that she's adopted. But when Pablo, a refugee from Milly's birth country, transfers to her school, she is forced to confront her true identity.

The Sisterhood of the Traveling Pants • Ann Brashares
978-0-385-73058-7
Over a few bags of cheese puffs, four girls decide to form a sisterhood and take the vow of the Sisterhood of the Traveling Pants. The
next morning, they say goodbye. And then the journey of the Pants,
and the most memorable summer of their lives, begin.

The Second Summer of the Sisterhood • Ann Brashares
978-0-385-73105-8
With a bit of last summer's sand in the pockets, the Traveling Pants
and the Sisterhood who wears them—Lena, Tibby, Bridget, and
Carmen—embark on their second summer together.

Girls in Pants: The Third Summer of the Sisterhood
Ann Brashares • 978-0-553-37593-0
It's the summer before the Sisterhood departs for college . . . their last
real summer together before they head off to start their grown-up
lives. It's the time when they need their Pants the most.

A Great and Terrible Beauty • Libba Bray • 978-0-385-73231-4
Sixteen-year-old Gemma Doyle is sent to the Spence Academy in
London after tragedy strikes her family in India. Lonely, guilt-ridden,
and prone to visions of the future that have an uncomfortable habit of
coming true, Gemma finds her reception a chilly one. But at Spence,
Gemma's power to attract the supernatural unfolds; she becomes
entangled with the school's most powerful girls and discovers her
mother's connection to a shadowy group called the Order. A curl-up-
under-the-covers Victorian gothic.

Rebel Angels • Libba Bray • 978-0-385-73341-0
Gemma Doyle is looking forward to a holiday from Spence Academy—spending time with her friends in the city, attending balls in fancy gowns with plunging necklines, and dallying with the handsome Simon Middleton. Yet amid these distractions, her visions intensify—visions of three girls in white, to whom something horrific has happened that only the realms can explain.

Walking Naked • Alyssa Brugman • 978-0-440-23832-4
Megan doesn't know a thing about Perdita, since she would never dream of talking to her. Only when the two girls are thrown together in detention does Megan begin to see Perdita as more than the school outcast. Slowly, Megan finds herself drawn into a challenging almost-friendship.

Colibrí • Ann Cameron • 978-0-440-42052-1
At age four, Colibrí was kidnapped from her parents in Guatemala City, and ever since then she's traveled with Uncle, who believes Colibrí will lead him to treasure. Danger mounts as Uncle grows desperate for his fortune—and as Colibrí grows daring in seeking her freedom.

The Chocolate War • Robert Cormier • 978-0-375-82987-1
Jerry Renault dares to disturb the universe in this groundbreaking and now classic novel, an unflinching portrait of corruption and cruelty in a boys' prep school.

Bud, Not Buddy • Christopher Paul Curtis • 978-0-553-49410-5
Ten-year-old Bud's momma never told him who his father was, but she left a clue: flyers advertising Herman E. Calloway and his famous band. Bud's got an idea that those flyers will lead him to his father. Once he decides to hit the road and find this mystery man, nothing can stop him.

Dr. Franklin's Island • Ann Halam • 978-0-440-23781-5
A plane crash leaves Semi, Miranda, and Arnie stranded on a tropical island, totally alone. Or so they think. Dr. Franklin is a mad scientist who has set up his laboratory on the island, and the three teens are perfect subjects for his frightening experiments in genetic engineering.

Keeper of the Night • Kimberly Willis Holt • 978-0-553-49441-9
Living on the island of Guam, a place lush with memories and tradition, young Isabel struggles to protect her family and cope with growing up after her mother's suicide.

When Zachary Beaver Came to Town • Kimberly Willis Holt
978-0-440-23841-6
Toby's small, sleepy Texas town is about to get a jolt with the arrival of Zachary Beaver, billed as the fattest boy in the world. Toby is in for a summer unlike any other—a summer sure to change his life.

The Parallel Universe of Liars • Kathleen Jeffrie Johnson
978-0-440-23852-2
Surrounded by superficiality, infidelity, and lies, Robin, a self-described chunk, isn't sure what to make of her hunky neighbor's sexual advances, or of the attention paid her by a new boy in town who seems to notice more than her body.

Ghost Boy • Iain Lawrence • 978-0-440-41668-5
Fourteen-year-old Harold Kline is an albino—an outcast. When the circus comes to town, Harold runs off to join it in hopes of discovering who he is and what he wants in life. Is he a circus freak or just a normal guy?

The Lightkeeper's Daughter • Iain Lawrence • 978-0-385-73127-0
Imagine growing up on a tiny island with no one but your family. For Squid McCrae, returning to the island after three years away unleashes a storm of bittersweet memories, revelations, and accusations surrounding her brother's death.

Girl, 15, Charming but Insane • Sue Limb • 978-0-385-73215-4
With her hilariously active imagination, Jess Jordan has a tendency to complicate her life, but now, as she's finally getting closer to her crush, she's determined to keep things under control. Readers will fall in love with Sue Limb's insanely optimistic heroine.

The Silent Boy • Lois Lowry • 978-0-440-41980-8
When tragedy strikes a small turn-of-the-century town, only Katy realizes what the gentle, silent boy did for his family. He meant to help, not harm. It didn't turn out that way.

Shades of Simon Gray • Joyce McDonald • 978-0-440-22804-2
Simon is the ideal teenager—smart, reliable, hardworking, trustworthy. Or is he? After Simon's car crashes into a tree and he slips into a coma, another portrait of him begins to emerge.

Zipped • Laura and Tom McNeal • 978-0-375-83098-3
In a suspenseful novel of betrayal, forgiveness, and first love, fifteen-year-old Mick Nichols opens an e-mail he was never meant to see—and learns a terrible secret.

Pool Boy • Michael Simmons • 978-0-385-73196-6
Brett Gerson is the kind of guy you love to hate—until his father is thrown in prison and Brett has to give up the good life. That's when some swimming pools enter his world and change everything.

Milkweed • Jerry Spinelli • 978-0-440-42005-7
He's a boy called Jew. Gypsy. Stopthief. Runt. He's a boy who lives in the streets of Warsaw. He's a boy who wants to be a Nazi someday, with tall, shiny jackboots of his own. Until the day that suddenly makes him change his mind—the day he realizes it's safest of all to be nobody.

Stargirl • Jerry Spinelli • 978-0-440-41677-7

Stargirl. From the day she arrives at quiet Mica High in a burst of color and sound, the hallways hum with the murmur of "Stargirl, Stargirl." The students are enchanted. Then they turn on her.

Shabanu: Daughter of the Wind • Suzanne Fisher Staples
978-0-440-23856-0

Life is both sweet and cruel to strong-willed young Shabanu, whose home is the windswept Cholistan Desert of Pakistan. She must reconcile her duty to her family and the stirrings of her own heart in this Newbery Honor–winning modern-day classic.

The Gospel According to Larry • Janet Tashjian
978-0-440-23792-1

Josh Swensen's virtual alter ego, Larry, becomes a huge media sensation. While it seems as if the whole world is trying to figure out Larry's true identity, Josh feels trapped inside his own creation.